WHISKEY
Secrets

A Whiskey and Lies Novel

BY
CARRIE ANN RYAN

Whiskey Secrets
A Whiskey and Lies Novel
By: Carrie Ann Ryan
© 2017 Carrie Ann Ryan
Print Edition
ISBN: 978-1-943123-83-4
Cover Art by Charity Hendry

All characters in this book are fiction and figments of the author's imagination.

For more information, please join Carrie Ann Ryan's MAILING LIST.
bit.ly/18aFEqP

To interact with Carrie Ann Ryan, you can join her FAN CLUB.
facebook.com/groups/CarrieAnnRyanFanClub

Author Highlights

Praise for Carrie Ann Ryan....

"Carrie Ann Ryan knows how to pull your heartstrings and make your pulse pound! Her wonderful Redwood Pack series will draw you in and keep you reading long into the night. I can't wait to see what comes next with the new generation, the Talons. Keep them coming, Carrie Ann!"

–Lara Adrian, New York Times bestselling author of
CRAVE THE NIGHT

"Carrie Ann Ryan never fails to draw readers in with passion, raw sensuality, and characters that pop off the page. Any book by Carrie Ann is an absolute treat."

–New York Times Bestselling Author J. Kenner

"With snarky humor, sizzling love scenes, and brilliant, imaginative worldbuilding, The Dante's Circle series reads as if Carrie Ann Ryan peeked at my personal wish list!"

–NYT Bestselling Author, Larissa Ione

"Carrie Ann Ryan writes sexy shifters in a world full of passionate happily-ever-afters."

–*New York Times* Bestselling Author Vivian Arend

"Carrie Ann's books are sexy with characters you can't help but love from page one. They are heat and heart blended to perfection."

–*New York Times* Bestselling Author Jayne Rylon

Carrie Ann Ryan's books are wickedly funny and deliciously hot, with plenty of twists to keep you guessing. They'll keep you up all night!"

–USA Today Bestselling Author Cari Quinn

"Once again, Carrie Ann Ryan knocks the Dante's Circle series out of the park. The queen of hot, sexy, enthralling paranormal romance, Carrie Ann is an author not to miss!"

–*New York Times* bestselling Author Marie Harte

Dedication

To Daniel.
You should be here to read this, and I hate that you aren't.
I'll miss you more with every passing day.

Acknowledgements

Whiskey Secrets was the first book where my husband and I sat down with my plot and deconstructed it. He had always been a part of Team Carrie Ann, but this was the first time that we worked on things together because he wanted to get to know my readers and my books even more. He had read a few of my other books and knew my characters pretty well since I talked about them so much, but this was the first one where I actually plotted *with* him.

I lost him while I was editing this book, and he never got to read the final version.

He'll never read these words.

While I would normally thank every single person who was a part of making my books come to life, for just this once, I'm going to mention only one man in my life, the one who was—is—part of my soul. The man I'll miss every single day of my life.

This book is for him. It was always going to be for him.

So, Daniel, I hope I did you proud.

~Carrie Ann

Whiskey Secrets

Sparks fly between a former cop-turned-bartender and his new innkeeper in the first installment of a Montgomery Ink spin-off series from NYT Bestselling Author Carrie Ann Ryan.

Dare Collins is a man who knows his whiskey and women—or at least that's what he tells himself. When his family decides to hire on a new innkeeper for the inn above his bar and restaurant, he's more than reluctant. Especially when he meets the new hire. But he'll soon find that he has no choice but to work with this city girl and accept her new ideas and the burning attraction between them.

Kenzie Owens left her old life and an abusive relationship behind her—or so she thought. She figures she'll be safe in Whiskey, Pennsylvania but after one look at her new boss, Dare Collins, she might still be in danger, or at least her heart. And when her past catches up with her despite her attempts to avoid it, it's more than her heart on the line. This time, it might mean her life.

1

***

S HOCKING PAIN SLAMMED into his skull and down his back. Dare Collins did his best not to scream in the middle of his own bar. He slowly stood up and rubbed the back of his head since he'd been distracted and hit it on the countertop. Since the thing was made of solid wood and thick as hell, he was surprised he hadn't given himself a concussion. But since he didn't see double, he had a feeling once his long night was over, he'd just have to make the throbbing go away with a glass of Macallan.

There was nothing better than a glass of smooth whiskey or an ice-cold mug of beer after a particularly long day. Which one Dare chose each night depended on not only his mood but also those around him. So was the life of a former cop turned bartender.

He had a feeling he'd be going for the whiskey and not a woman tonight—like most nights if he were honest. It had been a long day of inventory and no-show staff members. Meaning he had a headache from hell, and it looked as if he'd be working open to close when he truly didn't want to. But that's what happened when one was the owner of a bar and restaurant rather than just a manager or bartender—like he was with the Old Whiskey Restaurant and Bar.

It didn't help that his family had been in and out of the place all day for one reason or another—his brothers and parents either wanting something to eat or having a question that needed to be answered right away where a phone call or text wouldn't suffice. His mom and dad had mentioned more than once that he needed to be ready for their morning meeting, and he had a bad feeling in his gut about what that would mean for him later. But he pushed that from his thoughts because he was used to things in his life changing on a dime. He'd left the force for a reason, after all.

Enough of that.

He loved his family, he really did, but sometimes, they—his parents in particular—gave him a headache.

Since his mom and dad still ran the Old Whiskey Inn above his bar, they were constantly around, working their tails off at odd jobs that were far too hard for them at their ages, but they were all just trying to earn a living. When they weren't handling business for the inn, they were fixing problems upstairs that Dare wished they'd let him help with.

While he'd have preferred to call it a night and head back to his place a few blocks away, he knew that wouldn't happen tonight. Since his bartender, Rick, had called in sick at the last minute—as well as two of Dare's waitresses from the bar—Dare was pretty much screwed.

And if he wallowed just a little bit more, he might hear a tiny violin playing in his ear. He needed to get a grip and get over it. Working late and dealing with other people's mistakes was part of his job description, and he was usually fine with that.

Apparently, he was just a little off tonight. And since he knew himself well, he had a feeling it was because he was nearing the end of his time without his kid. Whenever he spent too many days away from Nathan, he acted like a crabby asshole. Thankfully, his weekend was coming up.

"Solving a hard math problem over there, or just daydreaming? Because that expression on your face looks like you're working your brain too hard. I'm surprised I don't see smoke coming out of your ears." Fox asked as he walked up to the bar, bringing Dare out of his thoughts. Dare had been pulling drafts and cleaning glasses mindlessly while in his head, but he was glad for the distraction, even if it annoyed him that he needed one.

Dare shook his head and flipped off his brother. "Suck me."

The bar was busy that night, so Fox sat down on one of the empty stools and grinned. "Nice way to greet your customers." He glanced over his shoulder before looking back at Dare and frowning. "Where are Rick and the rest of your staff?"

Dare barely held back a growl. "Out sick. Either there's really a twenty-four-hour stomach bug going around and I'm going to be screwed for the next couple of days, or they're all out on benders."

Fox cursed under his breath before hopping off his stool and going around the side of the large oak and maple bar to help out. That was Dare's family in a nutshell—they dropped everything whenever one of them needed help, and nobody even had to ask for it. Since Dare sucked at asking for help on a good day, he was glad that Fox knew what he needed without him having to say it.

Without asking, Fox pulled up a few drink orders and began mixing them with the skill of a long-time barkeep. Since Fox owned the small town newspaper—the Whiskey Chronicle— Dare was still surprised sometimes at how deft his younger brother was at working alongside him. Of course, even his parents, his older brother Loch, and his younger sister Tabby knew their way around the bar.

Just not as well as Dare did. Considering that this was *his* job, he was grateful for that.

He loved his family, his bar, and hell, he even loved his little town on the outskirts of Philly. Whiskey, Pennsylvania was like most other small towns in his state where some parts were new additions, and others were old stone buildings from the Revolutionary or Civil war eras with add-ons—like his.

And with a place called Whiskey, everyone attached the label where they could. Hence the town paper, his bar, and most of the other businesses around town. Only Loch's business really stood out with Loch's Security and Gym down the street, but that was just like Loch to be a little different yet still part of the town.

Whiskey had been named as such because of its old bootlegging days. It used to be called something else, but since Prohibition, the town had changed its name and cashed in on it. Whiskey was one of the last places in the country to keep Prohibition on the books, even with the nationwide decree. They'd fought to keep booze illegal, not for puritan reasons, but because their bootlegging market had helped the township thrive. Dare knew there was a lot more to it than that, but those were the stories the leaders told the tourists, and it helped with the flare.

Whiskey was located right on the Delaware River, so it overlooked New Jersey but was still on the Pennsylvania side of things. The main bridge that connected the two states through Whiskey and Ridge on the New Jersey side was one of the tourist spots for people to drive over and walk so they could be in two states at once while over the Delaware River.

Their town was steeped in history, and close enough to where George Washington had crossed the Delaware that they were able to gain revenue on the reenactments for the tourists, thus helping keep their town afloat.

The one main road through Whiskey that not only housed Loch's and Dare's businesses but also many of the other shops and restaurants in the area, was always jammed with cars and people looking for places to parallel park. Dare's personal parking lot for the bar and inn was a hot commodity.

And while he might like time to himself some days, he knew he wouldn't trade Whiskey's feel for any other place. They were a weird little town that was a mesh of history and newcomers, and he wouldn't trade it for the world. His sister Tabby might have moved out west and found her love and her place with the Montgomerys in Denver, but Dare knew he'd only ever find his home here.

Sure, he'd had a few flings in Denver when he visited his sister, but he knew they'd never be more than one night or two. Hell, he was the king of flings these days, and that was for good reason. He didn't need commitment or attachments beyond his family and his son, Nathan.

Time with Nathan's mom had proven that to him, after all.

"You're still daydreaming over there," Fox called out from the other side of the bar. "You okay?"

Dare nodded, frowning. "Yeah, I think I need more caffeine or something since my mind keeps wandering." He pasted on his trademark grin and went to help one of the new arrivals who'd taken a seat at the bar. Dare wasn't the broody one of the family—that honor went to Loch—and he hated when he acted like it.

"What can I get you?" he asked a young couple that had taken two empty seats at the bar. They had matching wedding bands on their fingers but looked to be in their early twenties.

He couldn't imagine being married that young. Hell, he'd never been married, and he was in his mid-thirties now. He hadn't married Monica even though she'd given him Nathan, and even now, he wasn't sure they'd have ever taken that step even if they had stayed together. She had Auggie now, and he had…well, he had his bar.

That wasn't depressing at all.

"Two Yuenglings please, draft if you have it," the guy said, smiling.

Dare nodded. "Gonna need to see your IDs, but I do have it on tap for you." As Yuengling was a Pennsylvania beer, not having it outside the bottle would be stupid even in a town that prided itself on whiskey.

The couple pulled out their IDs, and Dare checked them quickly. Since both were now the ripe age of twenty-two, he went to pull them their beers and set out their check since they weren't looking to run a tab.

Another woman with long, caramel brown hair with hints of red came to sit at the edge of the bar. Her hair lay in loose waves down her back and she had on a sexy-as-fuck green dress that draped over her body to showcase sexy curves and legs that seemed to go on forever. The garment didn't have sleeves so he could see the toned muscles in her arms work as she picked up a menu to look at it. When she looked up, she gave him a dismissive glance before focusing on the menu again. He held back a sigh. Not in the mood to deal with whatever that was about, he let Fox take care of her and put her from his mind. No use dealing with a woman who clearly didn't want him near, even if it were just to take a drink order. Funny, he usually had to speak to a female before making her want him out of the picture. At least, that's what he'd learned from Monica.

And why the hell was he thinking about his ex again? He usually only thought of her in passing when he was talking to Nathan or hanging out with his kid for the one weekend a month the custody agreement let Dare have him. Having been in a dangerous job and then becoming a bartender didn't look good to some lawyers it seemed, at least when Monica had fought for full custody after Nathan was born.

He pushed those thoughts from his mind, however, not in the mood to scare anyone with a scowl on his face by remembering how his ex had looked down on him for his occupation even though she'd been happy to slum it with him when it came to getting her rocks off.

Dare went through the motions of mixing a few more drinks before leaving Fox to tend to the bar so he could go check on the restaurant part of the building.

Since the place had originally been an old stone inn on both floors instead of just the top one, it was set up a little differently than most newer buildings around town. The bar was off to one side; the restaurant area where they served delicious, higher-end entrees and tapas was on the other. Most people needed a reservation to sit down and eat in the main restaurant area, but the bar also had seating for dinner, only their menu wasn't quite as extensive and ran closer to bar food.

In the past, he'd never imagined he would be running something like this, even though his parents had run a smaller version of it when he was a kid. But none of his siblings had been interested in taking over once his parents wanted to retire from the bar part and only run the inn. When Dare decided to leave the force only a few years in, he'd found his place here, however reluctantly.

Being a cop hadn't been for him, just like being in a relationship. He'd thought he would be able to do the former, but life had taken a turn, and he'd faced his mortality far sooner than he bargained for. Apparently, being a gruff, perpetually single bar owner was more his speed, and he was pretty damn good at it, too. Most days, anyway.

His house manager over on the restaurant side was running from one thing to another, but from the outside, no one would have noticed. Claire was just that good. She was in her early fifties and already a grandmother, but she didn't look a day over thirty-five with her smooth, dark skin and bright smile. Good genes and makeup did wonders—according to her anyway. He'd be damned if he'd say that. His mother and Tabby had taught him *something* over the years.

The restaurant was short-staffed but managing, and he was grateful he had Claire working long hours like he did. He oversaw it all, but he knew he couldn't have done it without her. After making sure she didn't need anything, he headed back to the bar to relieve Fox. The rush was finally dying down now, and his brother could just sit back and enjoy a beer since Dare knew he'd already worked a long day at the paper.

By the time the restaurant closed and the bar only held a few dwindling costumers, Dare was ready to go to bed and forget the whole lagging day. Of course, he still had to close out the two businesses and talk to both Fox and Loch since his older brother had shown up a few moments ago. Maybe he'd get them to help him close out so he wouldn't be here until midnight. He must be tired if the thought of closing out was too much for him.

"So, Rick didn't show, huh?" Loch asked as he stood up from his stool. His older brother started cleaning up beside Fox, and Dare held back a smile. He'd have to repay them in something other than beer, but he knew they were working alongside him because they were family and had the time; they weren't doing it for rewards.

"Nope. Shelly and Kayla didn't show up either." Dare resisted the urge to grind his teeth at that. "Thanks for helping. I'm exhausted and wasn't in the mood to deal with this all alone."

"That's what we're here for," Loch said with a shrug.

"By the way, you have any idea what this seven a.m. meeting tomorrow is about?" Fox asked after a moment. "They're putting Tabby on speaker phone for it and everything."

Dare let out a sigh. "I'm not in the mood to deal with any meeting that early. I have no idea what it's going to be about, but I have a bad feeling."

"Seems like they have an announcement." Loch sat back down on his stool and scrolled through his phone. He was constantly working or checking on his daughter, so his phone was strapped to him at all times. Misty had to be with Loch's best friend, Ainsley, since his brother worked that night. Ainsley helped out when Loch needed a night to work or see Dare. Loch had full custody of Misty, and being a single father wasn't easy.

Dare had a feeling no matter what his parents had to say, things were going to be rocky after the morning meeting. His parents were caring, helpful, and always wanted the best for their family. That also meant they tended to be slightly overbearing in the most loving way possible.

"Well, shit."

It looked like he'd go without whiskey *or* a woman tonight.

Of course, an image of the woman with gorgeous hair and that look of disdain filled his mind, and he held back a sigh. Once again, Dare was a glutton for punishment, even in his thoughts.

THE NEXT MORNING, he cupped his mug of coffee in his hands and prayed his eyes would stay open. He'd stupidly gotten caught up on paperwork the night before and was now running on about three hours of sleep.

Loch sat in one of the booths with Misty, watching as she colored in her coloring book. She was the same age as Nathan, which Dare always appreciated since the cousins could grow up like siblings—on weekends when Dare had Nathan that was. The two kids got along great, and he hoped that continued throughout the cootie phases kids seemed to get sporadically.

Fox sat next to Dare at one of the tables with his laptop open. Since his brother owned the town paper, he was always up-to-date on current events and was even now typing up something.

They had Dare's phone between them with Tabby on the other line, though she wasn't saying anything. Her fiancé, Alex, was probably near as well since those two seemed to be attached at the hip. Considering his future brother-in-law adored Tabby, Dare didn't mind that as much as he probably should have as a big brother.

The elder Collinses stood at the bar, smiles on their faces, yet Dare saw nervousness in their stances. He'd been a cop too long to miss it. They were up to something, and he had a feeling he wasn't going to like it.

"Just get it over with," Dare said, keeping his language decent—not only for Misty but also because his mother would still take him by the ear if he cursed in front of her.

But because his tone had bordered on rude, his mother still raised a brow, and he sighed. Yep, he had a really bad feeling about this.

"Good morning to you, too, Dare," Bob Collins said with a snort and shook his head. "Well, since you're all here, even our baby girl, Tabby—"

"Not a baby, Dad!" Tabby called out from the phone, and the rest of them laughed, breaking the tension slightly.

"Yeah, we're not babies," Misty put in, causing everyone to laugh even harder.

"Anyway," Barbara Collins said with a twinkle in her eye. "We have an announcement to make." She rolled her shoulders back, and Dare narrowed his eyes. "As you know, your father and I have been nearing the age of retirement for a while now, but we still wanted to run our inn as innkeepers rather that merely owners."

"Finally taking a vacation?" Dare asked. His parents worked far too hard and wouldn't let their kids help them. He'd done what he could by buying the bar from them when he retired from the force and then built the restaurant himself.

"If you'd let me finish, young man, I'd let you know," his mother said coolly, though there was still warmth in her eyes. That was his mother in a nutshell. She'd reprimand, but soothe the sting, too.

"Sorry," he mumbled, and Fox coughed to cover up a laugh. If Dare looked behind him, he figured he'd see Loch hiding a smile of his own.

Tabby laughed outright.

Damn little sisters.

"So, as I was saying, we've worked hard. But, lately, it seems like we've worked *too* hard." She looked over at his dad and smiled softly, taking her husband's hand. "It's time to make some changes around here."

Dare sat up straighter.

"We're retiring. Somewhat. The inn hasn't been doing as well as it did back when it was with your grandparents, and part of that is on the economy. But part of that is on us. What we want to do is renovate more and update the existing rooms and service. In order to do that and step back as innkeepers, we've hired a new person."

"You're kidding me, right?" Dare asked, frowning. "You can't just hire someone to take over and work in our building without even talking to us. And it's not like I have time to help her run it when she doesn't know how you like things."

"You won't be running it," Bob said calmly. "Not yet, anyway. Your mom and I haven't fully retired, and you know it. We've been running the inn for years, but now we want to step away. Something *you've* told us we should do. So, we hired someone. One who knows how to handle this kind of transition and will work with the construction crew and us. She has a lot of experience from working in Philly and New York and will be an asset."

Dare fisted his hands by his sides and blew out a breath. They had to be fucking kidding. "It sounds like you've done your research and already made your decision. Without asking us. Without asking *me*."

His mother gave him a sad look. "We've always wanted to do this, Dare, you know that."

"Yes. But you should have talked to us. And renovating like this? I didn't know you wanted to. We could have helped." He didn't know why he was so angry, but being kept out of the loop was probably most of it.

His father signed. "We've been looking into this for years, even before you came back to Whiskey and bought the bar from us. And while it may seem like this is out of the blue, we've been doing the research for a while. Yes, we should have told you, but everything came up all at once recently, and we wanted to show you the plans when we had details rather than get your hopes up and end up not doing it."

Dare just blinked. There was so much in that statement—in *all* of those statements—that he couldn't quite process it. And though he could have yelled about any of it just then, his mind fixed on the one thing that annoyed him the most.

"So, you're going to have some city girl come into *my* place and order me around? I don't think so."

"And why not? Have a problem with listening to women?"

Dare stiffened because that last part hadn't come from his family. No. He turned toward the voice. It had come from the woman he'd seen the night before in the green dress.

And because fate liked to fuck with him, he had a feeling he knew *exactly* who this person was.

Their newly hired innkeeper.

And new thorn in his side.

2

"AND WHY NOT? Have a problem with listening to women?"

Kenzie Owens raised her chin and did her best not to show her nerves. She used to be better at that, but then life had happened. Now, however, she would not display her fear in front of her new employers.

And since she had a new bout of rage filling her veins because of this *guy*, she found standing her ground a little easier to do than before. She was used to people not giving her a chance and looking at her if she were too pretty to have a brain cell in her head, but right then, she wanted to kick this little bartender's ass.

Not that there was anything *little* about Dare Collins. His wide shoulders filled out his black T-shirt fully, so the fabric strained around his muscles. His dark hair was cut short but still somehow made the blue of his eyes stand out. She'd seen him work the night before and knew he was good with his hands, and with his customers. He was taller than she was by a few inches if she didn't wear her heels, and moved with a prowling grace that she'd have admired if she didn't know who he was. He'd also smiled last night instead of scowling or looking broody—unlike he was doing now.

But, honestly, she couldn't quite blame him for the scowl, considering he'd had no idea what his parents were up to with their part of the building. But the brooding? Well, that would just have to go because there was no way she was going to deal with that while she worked at the Old Whiskey Inn. She needed this job and new chance at life, and there was no way she'd let this man ruin it for her.

She'd had enough of men standing in her way, thank you very much.

Dare mumbled under his breath in answer but didn't drop his gaze. Well, then.

"Kenzie," Barbara Collins said with a smile as she turned. "I'm glad you could make it this early."

As Kenzie currently resided in one of the small rooms upstairs, it hadn't been that much of a commute for her. After all, Barb and Bob had been the ones to move her into the place the day before so she could be close to her work and, eventually, turn her room into the innkeeper's apartment.

"It wasn't that far of a walk," Kenzie said with a smile. She looked around the room at the Collins family and nodded. "I can go back out if you need a moment to talk. I didn't mean to interrupt."

"Don't leave," Barb said as she walked up to Kenzie and took her hand. Kenzie did her best not to stiffen at the touch. This woman wouldn't hurt her, and Kenzie needed to get over her aversion to contact if she was going to keep this job. "Let me introduce you to the family at least, and then we can all talk logistics." She pointed over at the largest man of the three Collins brothers. "That's Lochlan, or Loch if you want to go with that, and his daughter, Misty."

The large man stood next to one of the booths in the bar and gave her a slight nod. He looked a little dangerous and like he wasn't a man of many words. But for some reason, even though he probably should have scared her, he didn't. It was most likely because of the little girl on her knees in the seat of the booth pressed against his side. Misty gave Kenzie a small wave before turning her face into Loch's hip and giggling.

Shy, Kenzie thought. She could relate.

"And this is Fox," Barb continued. "Tabby's on the phone next to his elbow."

"Hi!" a woman's voice said from the phone. "Sorry I can't shake your hand or anything."

Fox snorted and stood up, holding out his hand. "This is for Tabby I suppose." He winked and then leaned down to kiss her knuckles. "And that's from me."

Kenzie blinked then raised her brow as she pulled her hand away from him. "Thanks," she said dryly.

Loch let out a low chuckle as Fox shrugged and went back to his seat.

"What's happening?" Tabby asked. "Is Fox being a dork again?"

"As always," Dare replied.

"And this is Dare," Barb said, narrowing her eyes at her son. "And he's going to apologize for that remark he made as you walked into the room."

Kenzie held up her hand and shook her head. "No need. He didn't realize I was there, and all of this was thrown on him at the last minute, yes?" She looked directly at Dare and raised her chin again. "Since you own this part of the building, that means you and I will be working alongside each other for the time being. Let's not start off on the wrong foot, shall we?"

Dare stared at her for a long minute before letting out a breath. "We'll see." He turned to his parents as he stood up from his seat. "I need to go get some paperwork done. After you're through with this meeting, come find me in my office and show me what you have since it seems I have no say in this."

"Dare..." his mother began.

Dare held up his hand. "No. I need to think, and if I don't leave now, I'm going to say something I'll regret." He blew out a breath. "I know this is good for you, and I'm happy you're finally taking time for yourselves, but doing it behind our backs? Well, I just need to go. Okay?" And with that, he walked out without giving anyone another glance. The others watched him leave, mixed looks of disappointment and that familiar broodiness on their faces before they started up their conversations again. Kenzie watched as Loch kissed the top of his daughter's head before showing her a game on his tablet.

These people were a family, and they seemed beyond close, and now Kenzie was here to stand in the middle of that. Okay, maybe not the actual middle, but close enough, it seemed.

Before the others could ask her questions and bring her into their talk, she quietly walked out of the bar and toward the back of the building to the inn. There was an outdoor entrance as well, but since she was already inside, she stayed and went to the staircase.

"I'd apologize like my mother wants, but I'm not sure what I'd say."

She turned at the sound of Dare's voice, doing her best not to jump out of her skin. She hadn't been aware he was in the hall, and she was surprised that she hadn't screamed.

"First off, I'm not just some city girl, Mr. Collins. I have ten years of experience in hotels and inns, as well as five of those in management. I have a degree in hotel management, and another in business. I know what I'm doing, and I don't care to be called names simply because I'm not from this small town."

Dare tilted his head as he studied her. "You're from the city, hence…city girl. And you might know what you're doing when it comes to hotels and other inns, but here in Whiskey? I don't know you, and I don't know what the plans are for the Old Whiskey Inn. But since I happen to own the other part of this building and run both of my businesses here, forgive me if I'm a little pissed off that I didn't know what was happening with the other third of the building."

And this was why she hadn't agreed with Barb and Bob's decision to not tell their children right away about the changes they wanted to make to the inn. They'd wanted to go to others with plans and details so no one would have to worry about the what-ifs, and while Kenzie somewhat understood that stance, she'd seen the other side, as well. What Barb and Bob wanted to do might have worked if this family weren't so close. They'd wanted to ease the burden on their children but, instead, they had only caused anxiety and whatever else was to come.

"I understand that," she said after a moment. "And, frankly, I agree with you." She must have surprised him, because his eyes widened.

"You agree?"

She nodded. "I think your parents should have told you. This is a business, *and* you're family. The reasons they didn't are their own, and I'm sure once you give them a chance they'll try to explain it to you, but you have every right to be mad."

He opened his mouth to speak, but she cut him off.

"What you do *not* have the right to do is blame me for this. You also do not have a right to treat me like anything less than my position here dictates because you're throwing a tantrum. I might be new to Whiskey, and my job here may have surprised you, but you need to get over whatever attitude you have toward me."

Dare snorted. "Attitude? Who exactly are you talking about? Me, or you? Because I said *one* damn thing, and now I apparently have an attitude problem when it comes to you. But, lady? You're the one who walked in here with a stick up your ass and your chin raised like you were looking for a fight."

"Call me *lady* again and see what happens."

Something flashed in his eyes. "I just might."

Unnerved, she took a step back and immediately regretted it. She'd told herself she would never back down again, yet here she was, doing it once more because a man dared to look at her with heat in his gaze. Whether that flash was from anger or something else, she didn't know. All she knew was that she needed to get a handle on herself and get back to talking about work and not whatever the hell was going on just then.

"When you're ready to talk about what we have planned for the inn, let me know. Until then, I'll be up in my room, unpacking."

Dare frowned. "You're living here now?"

She nodded. "I moved in last night thanks to your parents. Eventually, I'll be making that room into the innkeeper's suite for myself or anyone who comes after me, but that won't be for a while since we're planning on making that the last of the construction so I can live here while working on the business side of things with your parents."

His jaw clenched. "Seems like you have it all planned out."

"No, not yet, but it will be. And, hopefully, with your help since we'll be neighbors." Damn Barb and Bob for putting her in this position, but like she'd said, they had their reasons and intentions.

"I don't live here, Red. I do everything *but* sleep here it seems most days, but we won't be neighbors. And you're not my innkeeper, you work for my parents."

Red? Her hair was *not* red, more of a caramel strawberry or something, yet that's the only nickname he could give her? It was marginally better than *lady*, but still. She ignored the rest of his statement since they were only going in circles, and she wasn't in the mood to deal with whatever drama he had going on right then. She had enough of that in her life, thank you.

"Whatever you tell yourself, barkeep. Now, if you'll excuse me, I have work to do, and I'm pretty sure you just told your family you have the same thing."

She turned and made it halfway up the stairs before he called out, "Why didn't you mention who you were last night?"

She froze. Ah, he recognized her. She'd been exhausted from the drive and hadn't even unpacked yet. Fox had served her but hadn't seemed to recall her. Dare, however, had seen her and dismissed her the night before yet, apparently, remembered her even in different clothes and a more professional hairstyle. Maybe he was just good at that since it was his job and not Fox's. Or maybe she was thinking too hard about things that truly didn't matter.

"Red?"

"Don't call me Red," she bit out. "I have a name. Use it."

"I will." *Eventually* or *maybe* was left unsaid. "You going to answer my question?"

"I knew your parents hadn't told you about the changes yet, and introductions would have only added more questions that weren't my place to answer. Now, if you'll excuse me." She turned away from him again, and this time didn't look back when he made a sound. She wasn't sure what he meant by it, and she didn't have time to care. She had lists of lists to work on, and Dare Collins wasn't on any of them.

And he never would be.

BY THE TIME lunch rolled around, she was starving and in need of food. While she could have walked down the main street of Whiskey and tried out any of the numerous restaurants and cafes dotting the small town, she wanted to get a sense of Old Whiskey Inn and what it had to offer. This would be her new home, after all, and she wanted to feel like she was part of it.

She'd never truly integrated into the big cities she'd lived in for so long. Yes, she'd liked her apartments and made a few fragile friendships along the way. But those were broken quickly once she was pulled away in a new direction and forced to cut ties with anyone who might have mattered. She'd walked in a fog of loneliness without ever truly understanding how and when it had happened.

But that was over. She would make a new life here in Whiskey. Somehow, she'd remember how to make friends and do her best to make Old Whiskey Inn a profitable and desirable business, and she'd assimilate herself into the town.

Somehow.

The restaurant downstairs wasn't open for lunch on weekdays, but the bar was open every day for lunch and dinner. She'd try out the other businesses soon, as well as the restaurant itself since she planned to make it a large part of the packages the inn offered. For now, however, she'd see how lunch did at Dare's bar.

Dare.

Well, hell, that didn't take long for him to enter her thoughts, did it?

She pushed him firmly from her mind and made her way into the bar area of the building. She'd seen it in full swing the night before and had been pleasantly surprised by not only the food but also the atmosphere. Dare and his family had put a lot of love and hard work into the place, and it showed from every angle.

The bar itself was a thick wood that looked as though it had weathered years of use but still shined almost like new. There were thickly cushioned stools surrounding it, and even little hooks screwed into the wood for women to hang their purses on. She hated when she had to hang her bag on her knee since she didn't want to hang it on the back of her chair or set it on the floor where it could get stolen or dirty easily. Booths lined the walls in rectangles and some half circles for the corners. The chairs and cushions were leather and well maintained and seemed to be of decent quality. This might be a bar, but it was a high-end one with no tears or stray fibers to be seen.

And since it was lunchtime, the blinds were open, letting the bright, mid-afternoon sun in, making the place look different than it had the night before. While the restaurant had white linen tablecloths and waitstaff with long aprons and collared shirts, the bar area went with bare, wooden tables that gave it a slightly less upscale look. All in all, the place worked. People who didn't want to sit down for a five-star meal or didn't want to make a reservation could walk in and have fantastic bar food and tapas. Not a bad deal all the way around. And if she had any say in it, the inn would use both establishments as touchstones—more than they already did. She had plans, she told herself, she just had to make sure the Collins family liked them.

Pulling herself out of work mode, she smiled at the pretty blonde at the hostess stand. She wore a black blouse and skirt and fit in with both the bar and restaurant. Kenzie knew hostesses worked both places but mostly in the restaurant areas since the bar tended to be first come, first served. However, the woman must have gotten the memo about the new tenant because she moved to seat her right away.

Interesting.

The hostess sat her at one of the tables since she'd already eaten at the bar itself, and she smiled at the younger woman. The girl looked barely old enough to work at a bar in the middle of a weekday, but what did Kenzie know about age anymore. *She* felt far older than her twenty-eight years, that was for sure.

She let out a breath and was looking over the menu trying to decide what she wanted to eat when her phone buzzed. Stiffly, she forced herself to check the readout, swallowing the bile that crept up her throat once she read the words.

Not today, Satan.

Only that mantra didn't make her feel better like it should have. Instead, she barely held back the shaking in her hands. She could do this, she reminded herself. She was strong, damn it. Things were different now.

They had to be.

"Kenzie? What's wrong? You went pale."

She looked up at Dare when she heard the worry in his words and forced a smile on her face, though she knew it was only an imitation of one.

"What? Oh, nothing's wrong. I'm just hungry I guess."

He looked like he didn't believe her, and frankly, she didn't believe herself. But there was no way she was going to tell him why she wanted to simultaneously hide under the table and run from the building at the same time. She'd never tell him, she'd never tell anyone.

No one could know.

That was her past, and no matter how hard she hid from it, she knew it would always be there. Waiting.

But no one could know.

No one.

3

D ARE WATCHED KENZIE fight with something within herself but knew there was nothing he could do if she weren't willing to share. The odd thing was, he wasn't sure why he cared at all. She'd said she was fine, and he should just take that at face value. It wasn't like he knew her. They weren't friends. There was no reason he should know she was lying to his face other than the fact that he was a former cop, and now a bartender.

But he *knew* she wasn't okay and was trying to hide it. And while a small part of him might want to find out why, he pushed that to the side. He shouldn't care. He didn't. And that was how it had to be.

"You decide on what you want to drink?" He knew he sounded gruff but hell if he could help it.

"Do you normally take everyone's orders even before the waitress can bring me my water?"

She sounded so damn snippy, yet part of him liked it. He wasn't going to comment on *which* part.

"No, but I figured since you already said you wanted to start off on the right foot, I'd come over and ask." He hadn't meant to come over at all, honestly. He'd figured Kayla could handle the table, but when he'd seen Kenzie react like she had to whatever she'd seen on her phone, he'd come right over. He hadn't liked the look on her face but knew it wasn't his place to push any more than he already had.

"Oh," she said after a moment and seemed to gather herself. "Well, can I just have some water and an iced tea? No lemon please." She looked down at the menu and nodded. "It's the same menu from dinner last night?"

Dare shook his head. "No, it's slightly different, fewer offerings and more geared toward bar food than the tapas we sell in the evenings. The weekend lunch menu is just like the night menu though since tourists are in more."

Kenzie nodded, her face set in concentration. "You sound like you know what you're doing."

Dare just stared at her when she looked up and winced. "Family's been at it for a while now, pretty sure we can handle the menu of our bar. I'll get Kayla over here to help you with your order."

"Sorry," she said quickly. "I didn't mean to sound like such a witch just then." She let out a breath, and Dare folded his arms over his chest. Kenzie rubbed him the wrong way, and he didn't know if it was because of her iciness or the fact that his parents had hired her without talking to the family first. Probably the latter if he were honest with himself, and that just annoyed him more.

"I'll send Kayla over." He started to turn, and Kenzie reached out and gripped his arm. He hadn't realized he'd been standing so close. He didn't pull away from her touch, but he wanted to. He hadn't been expecting the burn from a woman who'd basically just called herself ice.

"I'm sorry," she repeated, meeting his gaze. "I had a phone

call earlier that rattled me, but that's no excuse. I told you before that I wanted to get off on the right foot and I can't seem to find that with you."

Dare nodded. "Understood. Nevertheless, I'll send Kayla over so you can settle yourself or whatever you need since I seem to rattle you just as much as that phone call did." Since she unsettled him just as much, he figured he needed the space, too.

"Never as much as the phone call," she murmured before leaning back and dropping her hand from his arm. He didn't know what she meant by her words but, once again, he didn't question her. He didn't know her, and frankly, was still a little pissed off about her role in his building.

Without another word, he headed over to the bar and went back to work. They didn't serve as much liquor, wine, or beer during the day—especially on weekdays—but some liked a little liquid inspiration with their work lunch. But even if the bar didn't sell that much, they still sold enough food to justify being open the additional hours. If tourists heard about the place in some magazine, they loved that they could come in and eat without a reservation. Lunchtime worked just fine for them, that way, they could find other places to eat at night that had walk-ins.

He had no idea how he'd ended up in this business based on what he'd done before as an occupation, yet being the boss seemed to fit him. He'd been a patrol cop for only a few years and had a damn good partner while they patrolled the streets. Now, Jason was gone, and Dare had the pain in his shoulder to remind him of that loss every damn day.

Dare let out a breath and gripped the edge of the bar, willing those thoughts and memories from his mind. He'd been thinking about Jason far too often lately, and he knew it was because they were nearing the anniversary of Dare leaving the force after everything had changed. He'd come home from the hospital with a hole in his shoulder, and a metaphorical one in his heart, only to have his ex leave him soon after—still pregnant with Nathan.

Hell, it was no wonder he worked at a bar that served damn fine whiskey—including the same label they'd had back in the day. If he didn't fall into the bottle, he might as well sell the damn stuff.

With a sigh, he pushed through whatever funk was pissing him off that afternoon and went to do inventory. They weren't that busy yet, and he figured Kayla could handle things for a while since Rick had shown up for his shift. Both were a little pale, and he figured they'd truly had a twenty-four-hour bug instead of going off on a bender the night before, and he was grateful for that.

His phone buzzed, and he looked at the readout, seeing Jesse's name. He stiffened before hitting ignore. She'd leave another message, and one day, he'd get up the courage to see what his former partner's widow needed from him.

For now, he didn't have the strength to listen to the grief in her voice. That made him a coward, but Dare had never said he was anything else.

Fox showed up not too long after Dare had settled behind the bar and growled something under his breath. His younger brother was about as tall as Dare but was more slender. While Dare had muscle from trying to stay in shape, Fox had always been leaner, while Loch was a bit more on the bulkier side from pure muscle. Fox's hair was a bit shaggier than his brothers', too, his eyes a bit lighter.

According to his parents, Tabby was the sweet one, Fox the funny one, Dare the intense one, and Loch the quiet and brooding one. And if that didn't actually describe them perfectly most days, he didn't know what did.

"What was that?" Dare asked as he set coffee and water down near Fox's elbow on the bar. Fox lived and breathed coffee—even far into the night—so Dare didn't have to ask what his brother wanted.

"The office is giving me a headache, so I'm taking my working lunch here." Fox pinched the bridge of his nose before setting up his computer. "Why did I decide to own a newspaper again?"

Dare snorted. "Because you like being in everyone's business. You're good at it."

Fox flipped him off while looking at his screen. "I tell the people what they need to know."

"Whatever you need to tell yourself at night." Dare wasn't a fan of reporters, hadn't been when he was a cop, and it had flowed into his present, but Fox was one of the good ones. There had been an issue with the previous mayor, and Fox had been the one to uncover the story when the local police force couldn't do the job. Dare had been in Philly at the time working as a cop, but he'd heard all about it. Fox had gotten major flack from it, but in the end, the truth had won out.

"I tell myself lots of things," Fox murmured, and Dare frowned, not sure what his brother meant by that. "Can I have a cheeseburger? No veggies or anything that could be considered healthy."

Dare snorted. "That I can do for you. Fries?"

"With a side of ranch like usual."

Dare barely held back a shudder. How Fox could dip his fries into ranch, he didn't know, but at least he didn't have to eat it. Dare went over to the computer to put in Fox's order and glanced over at Kenzie's table. *Wrong move*, he thought as he met her gaze.

Wrong damn move.

She tilted her head and studied him before going back to her salad. He scowled and rang up Fox's order.

"Have the hots for the new innkeeper, do you?" Fox winked, leaning back on his stool. "I remember her from last night, you know. Nice tipper. Great smile."

Dare narrowed his eyes. "First, I don't have the hots for her. Secondly, keep your voice down. She's right behind you, dumbass."

Fox shrugged. "You sound a bit defensive. Want to talk about that?"

"Don't go all reporter on me. Drink your damn coffee and get to work before one of your reporters shows up and annoys you here instead of at the paper." And with that, Dare went back to his office and let Rick handle the rest of the lunch crowd. He had a mountain of paperwork to deal with, and he had a feeling it was only going to get harder once construction on the inn started and Kenzie and his parents got into the first phase of their plans.

Dare sank into his chair and rolled his shoulder, wincing as it ached. He'd have to be careful when he went to Loch's later that night for his workout. He'd slept on it wrong, and it hurt like hell. It didn't help that the scar tissue from years ago seemed to flare up with any kind of weather that wasn't a balmy seventy degrees. Considering that he lived in Pennsylvania and not Florida, it meant it *always* ached.

He was about twenty minutes into his work when Fox walked into the office with his phone to his ear.

"Yeah, Tabby, I'm with him now. I'll put you on speaker."

Dare sat up, worried. "What's wrong?"

"Nothing's wrong, big brother," Tabby said with a sigh. "One day, I'll call, and you'll all assume it's because I want to annoy you with my day and not because something horrible happened."

Dare met Fox's gaze and knew the other man was thinking the same thing as he was. Tabby had been through hell before thanks to a man who hadn't understood that he couldn't use his fists and intimidation to get what he wanted. Her fiancé, Alex, had saved her and then helped her learn to defend herself—something Dare and his brothers should have done, damn it.

"And now you and Fox are probably looking at each other and brooding," Tabby said over the phone, pulling Dare out of his thoughts. "Now, stop it, because I have happy news and good things to talk about, and I'd like to stay in this cheery mood, thank you."

"Sorry," the two men mumbled together, and Tabby snorted.

"Love you guys. Okay, so I called because I wanted to talk about the wedding. It's wedding central down here with three back-to-back weddings going on with the Montgomerys, but Alexander and I really hope you can make it down before the ceremony itself so we can all spend some time together. I know it's not going to be easy, and I truly appreciate that you're coming to Denver at all, but I'd love to spend time with my big brothers and their children. If possible."

She sounded so happy, but the hesitation in her tone made Dare wince. He, Fox, and Loch had gone down to Denver once as a group, but that had been to check up on her and Alex. They hadn't had a lot of time to just hang out since all three of them were forced to take time off when they really hadn't been able to. Dare had been down again to see Tabby himself over the past few months, but he hadn't stayed long. The Montgomerys had taken her in as one of their own, but Dare knew he and his brothers wanted to make sure she never forgot that she was a Collins first.

"I can make it work," Fox said. "I've already talked to the staff about it and I'm finding better ways to work remotely. So, however long you want me in Denver, I'm there."

"That makes me so happy," Tabby said, and Dare heard the smile in her voice. "I miss you guys so much."

"Then why did you move so far away?" Dare asked before clearing his throat. He hadn't meant to let so much gruffness into his tone.

"Dare."

He let out a breath and shook his head, though he knew she couldn't see him. "Sorry. I know Denver is your home now."

"He's just grumpy because he has a thing for the new innkeeper."

"Ooooh, really?" Tabby teased, and Dare ground his teeth.

Fox just grinned, and Dare flipped his brother off. As much as he loved his family, they were a bunch of busybodies.

"Stay out of it, Fox," Dare growled.

"Oh? Like how you stayed out of my relationship with Alexander?" Tabby asked, her voice sweet.

"That's different."

"Sure, honey, if that's what you think." Tabby laughed. "I can laugh about it now because I know you love me and I know Alexander loves me with every part of him. But I do have to say, I'm kind of sad that I'm not there to witness Dare and Kenzie."

"I'll make sure I write down all my notes for you." Fox winked at Dare, and Dare moved closer, wrapping his arm around Fox's neck. He squeezed slightly, and Fox let out a clearly fake cough.

"You were always my favorite brother," Tabby said with a laugh.

"I'm standing right here, Tabs," Dare growled out, though he was laughing, too. Damn, he missed his sister. While part of him was glad she'd found her happiness with Alex and had put her past behind her, the other part of him wanted her closer to the rest of the family. He needed to get out there more often to visit, but between work and his weekends with Nathan, it wasn't easy. Tabby flew out here more often than not because she wanted to know her nephew, and Dare was grateful that she understood that sometimes Dare couldn't do what he wanted to with his family.

"You're in third place right now, sadly," Tabby said, not at all sorry from how it sounded. "Loch sent me a drawing Misty made for me, so that puts him right above you in the standings."

Dare ignored the little pang in his heart. It wasn't Nathan's fault that he didn't have as much time to draw things for his aunt. Monica didn't let him send stuff like that since she didn't want to confuse her son—her words, not Dare's. Dare did his best to make sure Nathan knew he was loved by all members of his family, but it was hard when he only saw his kid once a month and wasn't allowed to talk with him on the phone as much as he wanted to either.

Dare had screwed up royally when he tried to fight for custody with Monica. Between her family money and his high-risk jobs, he hadn't had a chance. It hadn't helped that he and Monica weren't married. The courts had ruled in the mother's favor, and Dare was at risk of becoming a stranger to his son no matter how hard he tried not to let that happen.

Fox and Tabby were still talking wedding plans when his phone buzzed in his pocket. He took it out and read the screen, a frown marring his face. He met Fox's gaze and nodded toward the hallway so he could answer. His brother gave him a look but stood up, picking up his phone as he did.

"Hey, Tabs? I'm going to take you out to the hallway. Dare has a phone call." He squeezed Dare's shoulder as he walked out, and Dare sighed. That wasn't exactly what he'd meant, but it worked.

"Hey, Monica," Dare said as he answered. He heard Fox groan out in the hallway, and Dare held back a smile. The two of them had never gotten along, and their animosity had only grown once Nathan was born and Fox wasn't able to get to know his nephew as much as he would have liked.

"Dare." Monica sighed, and Dare did his best not to let any resentment or anger fill him at the sound of her voice. She'd thought she was doing what was best for her son at the time, and though Dare hated the outcome, he knew she was a good mother. He told himself that often so he didn't end up a bitter old man who couldn't get to know his own son.

"What's up?"

"Nathan has a birthday party coming up for a friend, and it's on your weekend. Can you take him to it, or will you need to be at your bar?"

He didn't like the way she said *bar*, but in the end, he didn't really care how she felt about his job. She'd known who he was when they got together, and though Nathan had been unplanned, they loved that kid. They just had to work to remain civil. Hell, Monica wasn't evil, she just wasn't someone he really liked anymore, and that was kind of sad. They'd liked each other well enough to have a child, and that should have been good enough.

"I can handle it," he said smoothly, though he was annoyed. He didn't get that much time with Nathan as it was, and now he was going to lose precious hours because of a birthday party. But if his kid was happy, that had to be enough.

"It's only three hours, and they won't need you to stay since they have all the parental supervision they need."

In other words, the parents were in Monica's tax bracket and not his. *Oh, well*, Dare thought. He owned two businesses and worked his ass off. If anyone had a problem with what he did for a living, they could jump off a bridge.

"Just get me the details and tell Nathan I'll call him tonight to read to him." Monica at least allowed him that, and he forced himself to be grateful.

Damn it, he hated how things had worked out, but he needed to stop complaining.

"Will do." She hung up without saying goodbye, and he wasn't surprised. She didn't like wasting words on him, and he really didn't want to draw out their conversations more than he had to anyway.

Monica was a good person and a good mom. That was all

that mattered. The fact that they didn't like each other anymore was just a byproduct of two people who were poorly suited.

Someone shuffled to the office doorway behind him, and Dare turned, expecting to see Fox. Only it wasn't his brother.

"What can I do for you, Red?"

Kenzie narrowed her eyes at him and put one hand on her hip. "I was going to take a walk down Main Street to get to know the town. Fox offered up your tour guide services, but I can see you're busy."

Dare pinched the bridge of his nose. Was it too early for a drink? Probably, but hell, today seemed like it was a day for surprises.

"Fox said I'd show you around?" Of course, his brother had. Meddling asshole.

"I can do it on my own, but since we said we'd start new…"

"Then consider me your official Whiskey tour guide."

And, apparently, today was a day for bad decisions, too. But he might as well figure out exactly who his new innkeeper was and what exactly he was going to do about her.

Because even though he didn't want change and didn't relish dealing with what Kenzie would bring to what he'd established, he couldn't help but want her.

And that just confused the hell out of him.

4

ONCE AGAIN, KENZIE had no idea if she was making the smartest of moves, but she wasn't about to back down now. Though it was September, the weather fluctuated between stifling humid and hot to downright chilly. Right now, it was a pleasant day where she didn't feel like she was walking through a wall of humidity, nor did she need a jacket. Between that and the bright sun and tiny dots of clouds above her, it was a pretty nice afternoon.

"This is the main drag for the town." Dare gestured at the street. "It's pretty much a straight line except for one part where it curves over the bridge. The creek below that only starts pumping real good after a storm or right when the run-off from the mountains begins to melt. Other than that, it's a decent trickle that tourists like for selfies."

As Kenzie herself had taken a selfie in front of the creek for her personal album of memories, she ignored the humor in his voice at the comment. She'd told herself she would start taking more photos and enjoy where she was and *who* she was now that she was free of everything that had held her back for so long.

"It's a beautiful town," she said simply, and she was being honest about that. Everyone took great care of their buildings and businesses. There were coffee shops, teahouses, bakeries, restaurants, antique shops, clothing stores, and a couple dozen other shops that catered to practically every need. Everything was unique and could only be found in Whiskey.

And now, she was part of it.

"It's home." Apparently, Dare wasn't a man of many words today.

They walked another block in easy silence, and Kenzie sighed. She hated feeling awkward.

"So, have you always lived here?"

He looked down at her and studied her face as they waited at the crosswalk. "No. I lived in Philly for a few years."

"Big city," she said dryly then immediately regretted it. Weren't they supposed to be friends now? Or at least friend*ly*?

He snorted before stuffing his hands into his pockets. She couldn't help but notice the way his forearms tightened at the movement. She shouldn't be noticing the man's arms, damn it. Nor should she think forearms were sexy.

She'd come to Whiskey for herself, and had sworn off men and relationships. That meant no more looking at Dare Collins' arms and the way he filled out his jeans.

"Sorry about that. Like I said, I had a rough night and took it out on you."

"You already apologized. Let's get back to the bar. I know you have to work, and I have paperwork to go over."

His jaw tightened as he studied her. "Starting already?"

She raised her chin and then cursed herself for doing so yet again in front of this man. He set her on edge, and she wasn't sure if it was because they kept bumping heads or because she found him attractive when she didn't want to.

"I'm here to help your parents, Dare, and to do a job."

"I know you are." He turned away from her, giving her his profile. "And I'm glad my parents are taking a step back to actually try and relax. I'm just not a fan of change. Hell, I hate it, and I hate surprises even more."

That, she could totally understand. "I hate surprises, too. As for change? Well, sometimes, change is good." She was living proof of that, wasn't she?

"That's true enough, but it doesn't mean I'm quick to like it." He stared at her, and she blinked at the intensity. There was something there, she thought, some heat she couldn't quite name, and it worried her. Was he attracted to her? Or was that flare because she represented that change he wasn't ready for?

Either way, it didn't matter; thinking too hard along those lines when it came to Dare wasn't something she could do.

"But I guess it doesn't matter, does it?" Dare continued. "As for your new job? I'll be around if you need help. I don't know everything about the inn since I have my own two business to handle, but I can probably at least point you in the right direction. And if you're looking for upgrades like you mentioned? Talk to Loch. I know he's family, but he's damn good at handyman work and carpentry when he puts his mind to it. He hasn't done much on the inn since our parents weren't ready to update yet, but Loch's good at what he does."

Surprised, she found herself nodding. She'd already heard from her new employers about Loch and how he could help, and she was glad to know that the family stood together no matter what.

"I'll keep that in mind."

"You do that, Red."

She rolled her eyes. "My name's Kenzie."

"I know. I like Red too, though. Plus, it's fun to see you get all rattled when I call you that."

And she found this man attractive? She was seriously losing it. It must just be the nonexistent heat talking. Once she was fully immersed in her new job and life, she wouldn't be thinking about Dare and those sexy forearms of his again.

At least, she hoped.

FOUR DAYS INTO her new job, and Kenzie felt a little more surefooted about her position as innkeeper. She worked alongside Barb and Bob during the day and worked on paperwork and package options in the evenings when she wasn't eating at the bar or the restaurant downstairs.

The inn made decent money and had good bookings weekly, but in time, she thought they could make it even better. And to top it all off, it would make it easier on the older Collins couple so they could fully retire. She'd loved working as an innkeeper in her past job, and even as a hotel manager. She'd told Dare the truth when she said she had the experience, yet she hadn't told him everything.

After she'd gotten married, David had pulled her away from her duties ever so slightly at first. In the end, she'd had to quit her job to make her husband happy. She hadn't known he was manipulating her at the time, and even though her therapist told her not to, she still blamed herself partly for leaving a job she loved.

But all of that was in the past now, she reminded herself.

Annoyed that she'd let her thoughts go that direction again, she stood up from her small desk in her new apartment and picked up her bag. She had a few more things to do for the day before she could find something for dinner and enjoy her evening, but in reality, as an innkeeper, she was never truly off duty. Soon, the Collinses would help her hire someone part-time that could take care of duties when Kenzie wasn't on shift, but that wouldn't be for a while yet. She wanted to get the hang of things, and for now, between her and the older couple, they had things covered.

She headed downstairs to the second floor where her small office was behind the registration desk. Since the bar and restaurant were on the first floor, everything inn related was located on the top two floors with a back staircase and an elevator to connect them.

All guests had already been checked in for the evening, and that meant that Kenzie only had to be on call if someone needed something. So far, however, the guests seemed pretty self-sufficient.

She was just about to pull up the next week's arrivals when her phone chirped. She swallowed hard when she saw the readout, but answered anyway. There was only one number she was truly avoiding, after all.

"Hello, Jeremy," she said, false cheer in her voice. She loved her brother, she truly did, but he was exhausting to talk to and, honestly, a reminder of a past she'd do better to forget. She and her brother had never truly been close when they were growing up, but as he was only eighteen months younger than she was, they'd been raised almost like twins.

Twins who were so completely different that most people wondered if they were related at all.

"Oh, good, your phone works. From the way David talks, it's as if you broke the damn thing since you never answer him."

Kenzie sighed and pinched the bridge of her nose. So it was going to be one of *those* calls, was it? Lucky her. If only she had a glass of wine in her hand, maybe she'd find a way to get through it. Damn her and her inability to completely ignore the last connection she had to family.

"What can I do for you, Jeremy?" She tried to keep her voice pleasant, but she couldn't help the sweat breaking out over her skin at the mention of David's name. She'd come so far, yet not far enough it seemed.

Though she'd been the one to introduce her brother to her ex-husband, she still couldn't quite believe how close the two of them had become during her marriage, or how hard Jeremy clung to the other man once Kenzie finally found the courage to leave him.

"You need to answer David's calls, sis. You can't keep hiding from your problems. You know that's not what our parents would have wanted. You took a vow, and you need to keep it. It's how we were raised."

Bile filled her throat, but she swallowed it back. She wasn't a woman who bowed down to her brother's accusations and petty manipulations anymore. Just once, she'd have liked him to call her to ask how she was doing, to just talk about their lives rather than what she'd left behind or asking for something since he'd never been denied anything growing up.

"I'm divorced." Finally. "I owe nothing to David and don't plan on answering his calls. Ever. So feel free not to talk about him with me again."

"I'm sorry you feel that way right now." He paused, and Kenzie set her jaw. He never listened to her. "I actually called for something other than that. I'm sorry for bringing David up."

No, he wasn't, and they both knew it. And now, Kenzie knew exactly why he'd called. Just once, she'd love for him to need her for something beyond her bank account. Just once.

"What do you need, Jeremy?" she asked, resigned. Somewhere, deep down, she knew her brother loved her, but sometimes it was hard to keep that tiny thread of hope in mind.

"Just a little to get me by, Ken," he said softly, using her childhood nickname that made her ache for what she'd never truly had. "I was up for a while and have a lead on how to make that even more, but I need to pay my rent in a couple of days."

None of this should have surprised her. It wasn't the first time her baby brother had called needing money because he'd had a little too much to drink and gambled away the money he'd said he set aside for bills. She'd said countless times that she would never help him again, stop enabling him, but she couldn't find a way to say no and keep saying it.

"Jeremy," she sighed.

"Just a little. I promise. I'll pay you back. You know I'm good for it."

He wasn't good for it, and they both knew it. But what could she do? He had a job, but he wasted away his paycheck on games and bets he couldn't afford. If she turned him away, he could lose everything and would only come to her for help. Or worse, resent her for pushing him away. And, ultimately, blame her.

He would never blame himself.

"I can't," she said, her voice breaking. "Not this time, Jeremy. I'm just starting this new job, and I don't have any extra money lying around." Not a lie, but not the reason she was saying no either. "And I helped you a few months ago. I shouldn't do it again. If you'd just save—"

"David was right about you, bitch," Jeremy spat before hanging up on her.

Kenzie closed her eyes, willing the tears away as she placed her cell back in her bag. She shouldn't have even bothered to answer the phone. She'd known going in that nothing good could come of it, but she hadn't been able to give up hope that there was a slim chance that Jeremy wanted to be more than he was.

Saying no to him hurt, and she knew he'd call in a few weeks to apologize, telling her that he hadn't meant to say those things and that everything had worked out in the end. Then, soon after, he'd call again, asking for money once more or berating her for leaving David after staying too long in a relationship that had slowly drained the life from her.

There was a creak of the wood floor behind her, and she turned, quickly wiping her eyes as she composed herself.

"Loch, sorry, can I do something for you?" The eldest Collins brother was wide with muscle, and had a scowl on his face most days unless he was looking at his daughter. She had spoken to Dare and Fox far more than she had Loch, even though she'd seen him more over the past two days than she had the others.

He not only owned a gym, but he also taught self-defense classes in the evenings—something she might look into once she found the courage. And when he wasn't doing that or taking care of Misty, he was working around the inn on the small things that needed to be fixed. She knew when the time came for more in-depth upgrades, he'd help her and his parents find a larger company, but for now, he was good with his hands.

Of course, that statement made her wonder if Dare was good

with his hands, and she firmly pushed that thought from her mind. She wasn't ready to start thinking about men that way, and her boss's son was definitely not a man she should even tempt fate thinking about.

Loch, leaning against the doorway, studied her a moment before shaking his head. "I was just coming in here for a pen, actually. Didn't mean to startle you. You okay, Kenzie?"

She nodded, hoping her tears had dried. She was through crying for things out of her control. "I'm fine. Let me find you that pen."

"Are you bothering the new innkeeper?" a voice asked from behind Loch. And before the man could answer, a slender woman with long, chestnut hair and a wide grin ducked under Loch's arm and stood by his side. "Hi, Kenzie. I'm Ainsley. Sorry it took me so long to come over and say hi. Work's been keeping me busy, and with back to school things, it's been a little insane."

Ainsley. The Collinses had mentioned the other woman. She was a family friend and, most importantly, Loch's best friend. Ainsley also taught high school chemistry and ninth-grade science at the local high school.

Kenzie held out her hand and shook the other woman's, smiling as she did. "It's so nice to finally meet you. Barb and Bob speak highly of you."

If possible, the other woman smiled even wider. "Good to know they're keeping the scary stuff hidden. Anyway, I was coming up here to see if you wanted to have a drink with me before your dinner. To welcome you to Whiskey."

The other woman bounced as she spoke and leaned into Loch ever so slightly. When she did, however, Loch stayed stock-still, not moving away from her touch but not leaning in closer either.

Interesting.

"You know, that sounds wonderful." And after the call she'd just had, it did. Before, she might have hidden away upstairs so she wouldn't have to deal with anyone, but that wasn't how she wanted to react now.

"I'll leave you both to it," Loch said roughly, taking a step back. He looked down at his watch and frowned. "I need to head over to pick up Misty. I'll finish up what I was working on tomorrow, Kenzie. Sorry I couldn't finish today."

"You're doing a hundred different things. I'm just glad you're able to do what you can." She didn't know where Loch found the energy, but she was grateful for it.

"You okay tonight with Misty?" Ainsley asked, her eyes on Loch's. "I can stop by later and watch her if you have work to do."

He shook his head. "We're good tonight. You do enough, Ains." And with that, he nodded at Kenzie before walking out, leaving the other woman looking not quite as bubbly as she had before.

"Have you had a taste of one of our whiskeys yet?" Ainsley asked, her smile bright again, but Kenzie had seen it dim ever so slightly when Loch left.

"You know, I haven't. And since I live in a town named for the famed drink, I should probably remedy that."

"I think that sounds like a plan. But since it's whiskey and not a single glass of wine, we'll probably have to order some tapas. Dare's working the bar tonight, so he'll do us right."

Dare. Of course, Dare's name would come up and set her

mind going in a direction she didn't want. Why did she keep thinking about him anyway? Just because she found him mildly attractive when she didn't find *anyone* good-looking these days didn't mean a thing.

The man was living up to his name. A dare.

Something she couldn't possibly take.

Ever.

5

"DAD! LOOK AT this!" Nathan ran over to Dare's side with something in his tiny, clenched fist, and a wide grin on his face. His kid looked just like Dare had when he was Nate's age, albeit with slightly shorter hair since Monica didn't like it hanging in Nate's face. But the two of them still had the same color eyes, same smile, and according to his mother, the same bundle of energy that sent them bouncing from one side of the house to the other.

And maybe it was because Dare didn't have as much time with Nathan as he wanted, but hell, he'd take every ounce of energy this kid had just so he could be near his son.

"What is it, Nate?" Dare asked as he crouched down so he was at eye level with his four-year-old.

Nate opened his hand to reveal a particularly smooth rock. "It's special. Right?"

Dare smiled and ran his hand through Nate's hair. "Yeah, it's pretty special all right. Want me to keep it safe for you while you play?"

"Yes, please." His kid beamed and handed the rock over to his dad before running back toward his toys in the small yard. Dare didn't have much, but he'd saved all he had to make sure Nate had a home to come to and call his when he wasn't at his mom's.

"Dare? Are you listening to me?" Monica asked from behind him, and Dare let out a sigh. She usually just dropped Nate off, but today, she'd had a few things she wanted to talk about, and that meant Dare had to listen to the subtle put-downs he was sure she didn't even realize she was giving him. She expected more from him because, apparently, he hadn't been the man she thought he was…and he couldn't quite blame her.

And he'd stand there and listen because to not do so meant he risked time with his son.

"Sorry, what was it you were saying?" he asked, his eyes on Nate as he put the rock into his pocket.

"I hope you aren't planning to let Nathan take that home with him after this weekend. He has so many rocks and shells from the beach in his room that they'll spill over into the hallway any moment."

Dare finally turned and looked over at Monica. She looked the same as she had for as long as he'd known her. Long, dark hair; big, green eyes; and a frown on her face when she caught sight of him.

Sigh.

"I'll keep it in his room here." He didn't bother to mention the word *home* when it came to Nate's bedroom in his place—at least not in front of Monica. That just made things awkward for everyone involved. His son knew he loved him, and that was all that should matter.

Monica's mouth twitched into smile. "Soon you're going to have those rocks and shells in your hallway, too."

Dare shrugged. "Either he'll grow out of it, or he'll end up a geologist. It's what kids do."

"True," Monica said softly. "So, I wanted to talk to you about Christmas."

Frowning, Dare turned. "What about Christmas? It's my year, right?" They alternated holidays according to the custody agreement, and he wasn't about to lose time with Nate.

Monica bit her lip. "You see, Auggie's work wants to send him to Paris for a conference over the holidays, and he wants his family with him. They're doing a whole event there with games and parties for the children. It will be really good for Auggie's place at the company to have us there."

Dare's jaw set. "He's my son, Monica. Auggie's a good step-dad, but *I'm* Nate's father."

She blew out a breath and started pacing. "I get that, Dare. But Nathan spends more time with Auggie than he does you."

"And whose fault is that?" Dare bit out. "Don't throw my lack of time with my son in my face, Monica. Not when you're the one who took him away from me."

"The courts chose best, Dare."

"Fuck that," he whispered, not wanting Nate to hear him. "Don't come at me with that. And if you want your husband to look good for his big bosses, then you go. But Nathan is staying with *me* this Christmas like we agreed. It's *my* holiday. My parents are already planning a big family event, and it's still months away. Don't fight me on this. Don't take away my son."

Fire came into her eyes, and she curled her lip before she masked her emotions as she normally did. "We'll see."

And with that, she went to Nate's side and kissed the top of his head before striding out of Dare's backyard without another word.

"Jesus Christ," Dare muttered, pissed off all over again at

what his life had turned into. He might not be a cop anymore, putting his life on the line but, apparently, he still wasn't good enough to be a full-time dad.

He'd been a cop for four years before he was shot in the shoulder and lost his partner all in one night. Monica had been three months pregnant at the time and hadn't stayed by his side through his recovery or his grief. His brothers and the people he'd worked with at the precinct had never forgiven her, and hell, he wasn't sure he could either. Yes, she'd hated his job and loathed what it had done to their relationship, but she'd left him and taken Nate with her. She'd used her family money, and a high-powered lawyer, to get what *she'd* thought would be best for their son and had left him with almost nothing to hold onto when he recovered.

He'd never forgive himself—or Monica for that matter—for what had become of his relationship with his kid.

"Daddy?" Nate asked from his side. "Are you sad?"

Dare pushed out the thoughts of failure and whatever else Monica brought with her and shook his head. "No, not really." He didn't want to lie to Nate, but sometimes he had to be careful with what he said so he didn't hurt the little guy without thinking. "Just worrying about little things I shouldn't. Not when I could be playing with you."

Nate beamed and tugged at Dare's hand, and soon, the two were embroiled in a foam gun battle between monsters and aliens, all thoughts of what could have been long forgotten.

"WHAT DO YOU want for lunch, kid?" Dare asked as he settled Nate into one of the booths at the bar. Misty sat on the other side with Ainsley, her coloring book open in front of her as she pulled out her crayons for her and Nate to play with. Dare would never let memories like this fade from his mind and knew he'd do whatever he could to have more of them.

"Hot dogs!" Nate shouted, and Dare sighed.

"Inside voice, Nate." He winked when Nate blushed and wiggled in his seat. "And you can have a hot dog, but then you have to have apple slices on the side."

"Okay. If I have to." Nate gave a dramatic sigh, and Dare did his best not to laugh and encourage the little stinker.

"I like apples," Misty said sweetly.

"Of course, you do," Ainsley said as she leaned back in her seat. "Fruit is like dessert they let you have all the time. So, really, you have dessert on the side of your meal." She looked up at Dare and smiled. "Are you taking all of our orders for Rick, or should I go up there myself? I don't want to bother Shelly or Kayla since they're so busy."

Dare glanced over his shoulder and looked around the full bar. They had families and singles at each table, and there was a wait group that made his business owner-self happy. Kayla and Shelly were busy but not running around like crazy. If they needed him, they'd let him know. The last time he'd tried to step in on his afternoon off, he'd gotten shoved out of the way and called a micromanager. He knew better now. Somewhat.

"I'll take it up to Rick," he said finally, keeping his eyes on his bar. "I'm not working tonight, obviously, but I still like to come in and check in, you know?" He didn't work on the weekends he had Nathan and trusted Rick and the rest of his staff to handle the place for those two nights of the month.

"Thank you!" Ainsley told him her order before she leaned over to hand Misty another crayon. She was so good with that little girl, and Dare still sometimes wondered why she wasn't with Loch even though they were best friends. He'd thought they might be something more, but what did he know.

As he walked back to the booth, Kenzie walked into the bar area, a stack of leather folders in her arms and reading glasses on the tip of her nose. Her hair flowed around her shoulders and down her back, and he realized it was the first time he'd seen her hair down since that first night in the bar. And he had to say, he liked it better this way. He could imagine it wrapped around his fist as he…

Okay, enough of that.

He might find her attractive, but there was no way he would act on it. They worked together, sort of, and they were just now figuring out how not to be awkward and weird around each.

"Kenzie!" Ainsley called. "Come over here."

Dare watched as surprise crossed Kenzie's features before she schooled them and smiled softly over at the booth. He grabbed his and Nate's drinks and headed over, walking alongside her.

"Hey, Kenzie."

"Dare, I thought you were off today."

"I am, but I like to come into the place for lunch when I have Nate." He set the drinks down on the table and gestured toward his son. "Nate, meet Kenzie, our new innkeeper. Kenzie, this is my son, Nate."

"Hi," Nate said quickly before turning back to his coloring with Misty.

"Hey there," Kenzie said and shifted her weight while still holding those thick binders.

"Here, let me take those," Dare said, pulling the leather folders from her arms. Their skin brushed, and he did his best not to react. His attraction to her was dangerous and a distraction.

"Thanks," she said with a smile.

"Take a seat, Kenzie," Ainsley said as she scooted over. "There's plenty of room since this is technically a six-top. We just take it since it's in the back corner and not near a big window. That leaves the other spots open for the tourists."

"Oh, I couldn't," Kenzie said, taking a step back, but Dare put his hand on the small of her back to steady her.

Mistake.

"Come on, there's room, and you came down here for a reason, didn't you?" Dare said softly.

Kenzie shook her head. "I was just going to sit at the bar and catch up on some paperwork while I ate."

"Then sit here and do it with us," Ainsley urged. "Come on, get to know the rest of the Collins family."

Misty leaned around Ainsley and held out a crayon. "You can help us color if you want. Nate likes blue though, so you'll have to use green."

"Blue's the best color," Nate said as he bent over his page, his little face a mask of concentration. "But I like pink, too. It's pretty."

"Because pink isn't a girl color. That's just what the media tells you to think." Misty said it so matter-of-factly that it took Dare a minute to comprehend that she had to be mimicking something someone else had said word for word. Not that he didn't totally agree with the idea, but he had a feeling he knew who had taught Misty that phrase.

Dare and Kenzie laughed together as they sat down on opposite ends of the booth while Ainsley blushed.

"It's true," Kenzie agreed. "And I'm very happy you think that way."

Misty beamed. "Ainsley teaches me lots of things."

"I'd say she does," Dare murmured, and Ainsley shot him a look. "Does Loch know that his daughter's a proud feminist?"

"Of course. He's one, too, darn it." Ainsley winked before leaning into Kenzie's shoulder. "So, how are you liking Whiskey now that you're a little more settled?"

Dare didn't know when the two of them had become friendly, but he was glad. Not only did Kenzie have a friend here now, but Ainsley also had a girlfriend. Between work and Misty, Dare wasn't sure Ainsley had many friends outside of Loch and the rest of the family.

"I'm still settling, but Whiskey is a wonderful place," Kenzie said softly. "I feel like it could be home, you know?" There was something almost wistful in her voice, and Dare wondered what that was all about. He didn't know who exactly this woman was, but he knew she had secrets.

Hell, they all had secrets, things they'd rather others not know. But with Kenzie? Dare had a feeling it was something more. Maybe if he were still a cop, he'd want to dive into that even deeper, but since he wasn't, he told himself he'd give her space. She had a right to what she wanted and needed to keep to herself, and hell, who was he to pry, especially when he told himself there needed to be boundaries.

Kenzie's leg brushed his, and they both stiffened before Dare forced himself to relax. Ainsley raised a brow as she looked between the two of them, and he cleared his throat.

"So, uh, what did you want for lunch? I'll go and order it for you."

"I got the hot dogs," Nate said as he looked up from his coloring book. "But I have to have apples instead of friend fries."

Kenzie smiled at Nate and leaned forward. "I like hot dogs, too, but I think today I'll have the salad." She quickly looked down at her menu. "In fact, I think your dad has a salad with apples, right?"

He nodded, a smile slowly spreading over his face. "We do. Let me go add it to our order. One sec."

Dare quickly got up, careful to avoid touching Kenzie again, and made his way to the bar to add her order. He didn't know what it was about being around her, but he lost the ability to speak. He sounded off and grunted more than he used words— something so unlike him, it wasn't funny.

He needed to keep his head on his work and his son and nothing else. His family needed him, and he had his sister's wedding coming up. Thinking dirty thoughts about the new innkeeper wouldn't do him any good.

No matter how sexy she looked with her hair down.

6

KENZIE MOANED, ARCHING up into the man above her as he lowered his head to take her breast into his mouth. His tongue lapped at her nipple before he bit down gently, sending a shock through her system. She wrapped her legs around his hips, urging him closer. She was so close, *so* close to finally coming, yet he wouldn't fill her, wouldn't stretch her and pump into her until they both came, screaming each other's names.

Her lover sucked on her other nipple before moving up to take her mouth with his. That was when she noticed his face. It took a moment for it to come into focus, and by that time, she was moaning, her breasts pressed firmly against his chest.

But she knew the features.

Knew this man.

And realized this must be a dream.

But she didn't wake up. Instead, she held Dare closer, her mouth parting as he entered her slowly, inch by inch. Soon, they were clawing at one another, trying to pull each other closer as they crested their peak, their bodies sweat-slick and aching.

Yet when she tried to open her eyes to see his face one more time, he was gone. Instead, she stood in the center of her living room. No, not *her* living room. Not anymore. Those weren't her dark brown curtains. That wasn't her rug with the frayed edge that had caused so many tears.

This wasn't her home any longer.

But *he* was here.

Hands wrapped around her upper arms as she screamed.

Kenzie found herself sitting straight up in her bed, sweat sliding between her breasts as her sheets pooled around her waist. Her chest rose and fell in heaving pants as she fought to catch her breath and try to understand her nightmare and why she would dream it in the first place.

David had only touched her the one time in anger. He'd been much smarter than that before he finally lost his temper and broke her will. He'd used his words and taunts to break her down little by little before then. But he'd only taken her by the arms and shaken her that once. He'd only hit her that one time.

And that had been enough.

Finally.

She didn't know why she dreamed about it now. It had been long enough ago, and through therapy and distance, she'd hoped she had given herself time to heal. Only she had a feeling she knew why it had come back to her now and why those thoughts might never go away.

David may have only touched her once in anger, but Dare had never touched her with any emotion at all. A gentle meeting of skin here or there as they worked in the same building or ate food at the same table, but that was the gist of it. It was all there ever could be.

He was her boss's son for one thing. They worked in the same building for another. And he was far too dangerous for her. She'd seen the darkness in his eyes when his brothers mentioned what he'd done before he bought out the bar. To be safe, really *safe*, she couldn't touch that darkness, no matter how the embers burned and begged her to.

Kenzie ran a hand through her long hair, cursing herself for not at least braiding it the night before. Now she'd have to wash it again because it was so tangled. David had always liked her hair cut in layers around her shoulders or even shorter, and she'd never liked it that way. He'd somehow convinced her to keep it the length he preferred once because, after all, what was a small haircut to make her husband happy? But then when she'd tried to keep it long since her hair grew far too fast thanks to genetics, he'd manipulated her into getting it cut to the length he preferred again.

She could still hear his arguments. "No man in my position can allow his wife to look like a prostitute, Kenzie... Only women who are truly needy must have their hair so long that it could only be extensions... There can be nothing fake about you, Kenzie. You must look like porcelain, but *real*."

She'd cried the time he took shears to her hair as she slept, only to wake to the hacked-off ends near her cheekbones. Her hair had lain flat and lifeless, but she'd found a way to style it lest David get angry again.

Now her hair ran down her back and was almost unruly to handle. She'd spent far too much on a blow dryer that could tackle her hair in less than ten minutes, and whatever she didn't save from her paycheck for her savings account went to hair products.

But they were *hers*.

Kenzie let out a breath and slid out of bed, stretching her arms over her head while she walked toward her desk, picking up her phone and unplugging it from her nightstand along the way.

It was just after five a.m. and only twenty minutes or so before her alarm, so it looked like she'd get an early start.

On deck for the day was a few check-ins, talking to Loch about minor repairs and what could be done for a larger upgrade, and a meeting with Barb and Bob, who wanted to hire an assistant innkeeper. The latter made her smile with relief. The two of them together could handle the place on their own, though they'd gone through a few assistants in their time. Most of them had quit to move to bigger cities or had started families and didn't want to keep the position. Kenzie could understand both reasons for why the others no longer wanted the job, but the inn was her place and home for now.

She wasn't going anywhere, and now that she understood where Dare had been coming from that first day, she knew that no one wanted her to leave either.

It was an odd feeling—to be wanted, needed.

She just hoped she didn't prove them wrong.

LATER THAT EVENING, Kenzie sat at her desk in her office, looking over the files of the two people Bob and Barb thought would be perfect for the assistant job. And while they both had great qualifications and would probably be a wonderful fit, the elder couple had left the final decision up to Kenzie since she'd be the one working with the person and training them. It was a heavy responsibility, and she was honestly exhilarated and frightened all at the same time over it.

She was just about to get up for another cup of coffee when someone knocked on the doorframe. Her heartbeat sped up in her chest at the sudden intrusion, and when she turned to see who it was, her pulse only increased—and not in any way she could ever want.

"Jeremy. What are you doing here?" *How did you find me?* Though it wasn't as if she'd changed her name, was it? The divorce might be final, but she hadn't run away completely. David and Jeremy could find her at any moment, and this was proof.

Oh, God, she hoped David never showed.

He couldn't.

He *couldn't.*

"Can't I visit my big sister?" he asked, a frown on his face. "Nice digs. Though I still don't know why you want to clean up after people when you could have had better with David."

Kenzie scowled and walked past him, pushing him into the room so she could close the door behind him. "Jeremy," she hissed. "I work here. Watch what you say. I don't want any of the guests hearing you."

"Whatever." He shrugged and looked around her small office. It hadn't looked that little before, but with the reminder of her past standing in it, it looked much smaller now. Damn him.

"What do you want?" She kept her voice low and tried not to put her impatience in her tone. Jeremy could be as mean as David if he put his mind to it.

He narrowed his eyes. "We didn't finish our conversation. I got by last month, but this month will be too tight."

She raised her chin, steeling herself. "No, Jeremy. I told you, I can't help you. You're an adult now, and I have to stop enabling you. You can get a job and pay your rent. No one is making you gamble and drink your money away. You can get help."

"I'm *asking* you for help." He stalked closer, but she didn't back down.

"I can't help you the way you need."

His hands gripped her upper arms so much like in her dream she froze. "You bitch."

"What the fuck is going on in here?"

Jeremy let her go quickly, backing away as if he hadn't just threatened her. Kenzie was too shocked to say anything as Dare rounded on her little brother, rage in his eyes. She tried to catch her breath, tried to explain, but the words couldn't come.

"Who the hell are you, and why the fuck did you have your hands on Kenzie?" Dare was far bigger than Jeremy, but her little brother didn't back down. He'd never been in a fight with anyone, had never lost anything except money. He had no reason to be scared. No one had ever hurt him in his life.

And she wasn't about to let Dare do it now. Not because Jeremy didn't deserve it, but because *Dare* didn't deserve more darkness, no matter where it came from.

"Dare," she bit out, her hands icy cold at her sides. "This is my brother. He was just leaving."

That must have startled him because Dare stopped moving forward and looked over his shoulder at her. "Brother?"

She nodded tightly. "And he's *leaving*." She gave Jeremy a pointed look, and her brother huffed out of the room without a backwards glance, but somehow found a way to ram his shoulder into Dare's on his way out.

When Dare moved as if to go after him, Kenzie put her hand on his arm. "Please. Don't."

"What happened in here?" he asked, his voice a growl. "What did he do?"

"It was just a misunderstanding."

"Kenzie. I was a cop. I know better than that."

"He wouldn't have...he couldn't have..." She let out a breath. "He's never laid a hand on me before, and the fact that he even held my arms like that startled me. That's why I didn't move out of the way." *Partly.* "Thank you for coming in when you did. I'd like to think I'd have found a way out of whatever was going on without you, but...thank you."

Dare reached up as if to cup her cheek, and she backed away. She didn't know if she could handle his touch just then—and not just because of the anger that had filled the room before.

She didn't miss the hurt in Dare's gaze that he quickly masked.

Damn it.

"Glad you're all right, but if I see him coming up the stairs again, I'm kicking him out. You get me?" He didn't move to touch her, but his gaze was a brand nonetheless.

"I get you," she answered with a sigh. "I'm sorry you had to see my family laundry aired this way." And he hadn't even seen the worst of it, had he?

"You saw me make an ass of myself with my family when you first walked into this place. It's okay, Kenzie. Not your fault."

They stared at each other for a moment, an awkward silence settling over them.

"Oh, what did you need when you came up here?" she asked, trying to fill the void with conversation.

Dare look confused for a moment before shaking his head. "Ainsley is downstairs, and my brothers are on their way. They're doing whiskey flights and eating as a group. I have to work the bar since Rick is off, but they wanted you to come down and join them. Mom and Dad have Misty for the night since they're forcing Loch to socialize." He smiled as he talked about his family, and Kenzie couldn't help but feel just a bit wistful at it.

She had a mountain of work, and her hands still shook a little when she thought of what could have happened if Dare hadn't come up to the office when he had, but a night out sounded like something she could desperately use.

"That sounds like a blast," she said with a smile.

Dare studied her face as if looking for answers she wasn't willing to give. He nodded once and then walked out, leaving her alone in her office, feeling as though she was once again at a crossroads she couldn't quite figure out.

"One step forward," Kenzie reminded herself. One step forward. And, hopefully…no steps back.

"SO THIS IS the bourbon flight," Fox explained. "Whiskey is a large term for many types, but really, the main two you need to know are—"

"Scotch and bourbon. I know." Kenzie laughed as Loch rolled his eyes beside Fox.

"The guy's a reporter. He explains things for a living." Ainsley bounced on her stool and pointed at each glass on the wooden tray in front of her. "We're going American tonight, so no scotch, which is just fine with me."

"Sacrilege," Loch said, winking at his best friend.

Ainsley, in turn, flipped him off and held up a glass. "We're going from light to full-bodied. Sip, then swallow. This is to be savored, not taken like tequila." She narrowed her eyes as the two men gave each other looks. "It's also not like giving head where the man tells you he loves that you swallow and that's how you *prove* your love. Then you spit."

Kenzie threw her head back and laughed as the guys joined her. Dear Lord, she loved these people and was *so* damn glad Ainsley had invited her down for the night. She wasn't sure she'd ever had so much fun in her life.

"Do men really tell you that?" Fox said, wiping a tear from his eye. "Because, darling, I know you're not gullible."

"Damn straight," Ainsley said with a raised brow. "Why are you looking at me like that?" she asked Loch, and Kenzie turned to see what the man was doing.

He just frowned over at the group of them and shook his head. "Let's just drink our whiskey and not talk about shit like that."

Ainsley snorted. "What? Don't like thinking about me with a dick in my mouth?"

Fox winced and took the glass from Ainsley's hand. "And that's enough booze for you."

Considering they were on their second flight of whiskey as a group, Kenzie didn't disagree.

"Seriously? You two talk about dicks way more than I do." The other woman wasn't yelling or even talking loudly, but they weren't alone in the bar either.

"I'm taking you home," Loch said firmly as he slid off his stool. "It's late anyway."

Kenzie could see the fight in the other woman's eyes and knew she needed to stop it. "I'm tired," she said, not lying. "We can do this other flight another day. How's that? That way, we don't do everything at once."

Ainsley narrowed her eyes at her but sighed. "Fine. But I can walk home."

"Not alone, you won't." Loch folded his arms over his chest and looked every bit the man who owned a gym and security company.

"The lady doesn't need your help," a slurred voice said from behind them. "Why don't I take her off your hands."

Kenzie stiffened and looked over her shoulder as two clearly drunk men came over to their end of the bar.

"Shit," Fox whispered and tugged Kenzie behind him ever so slightly.

"Okay, fellas, we're just hanging out with our friends tonight," Fox put in. "This is a classy place, let's not get into trouble."

"Maybe we want trouble," the other man slurred, his eyes going dark.

"Thanks for the offer, but I'm good," Ainsley said, not a hint of liquor in her eyes.

"Is there a problem here?" Dare asked as he slid out from behind the bar. "Why don't we all sit down and let everyone enjoy their night?"

"Why don't you go fuck yourself?" the first drunk barked back before swinging a fist in Fox's direction.

Fox ducked, bringing Kenzie with him, and she fell to her knees, her palms slapping the hardwood.

"Fuck," Dare growled out and picked her up, swinging her behind him. "Stay there," he ordered as he went into the fray.

Ainsley grabbed Kenzie's wrist and squeezed. "Let the guys handle it this time. They will deal with it a lot faster if we stay out of the way. Loch taught me to protect myself, but the first thing I learned is not to get in the middle of a group of guys larger than you with fists flying." She paused. "I didn't mean to make them all fight."

Kenzie shook her head, memories of shouted words and fists slamming into her. "It's not your fault."

"They don't usually have fights like this in the bar. We're not that kind of place, you know?" Ainsley whispered, but Kenzie could only keep her eyes on Dare.

Three drunk men came at the Collins brothers, but they were no match for them. Loch had one man on his knees in an instant while Fox had the other by the back of his neck, and Dare had a third on the floor beneath his boot. It was all over so fast, Kenzie had missed most of what happened...but she'd heard it.

Bile filled her throat once again, and when Dare turned to look at her, he cursed.

"Loch, take these guys outside for me, will you? Fox, join him." He turned quickly to the others in the bar. "Sorry about that. Just taking out the trash. Everyone gets a round on me."

The patrons cheered and went back to enjoying their nights, as if random fights like this happened in their lives all the time. Yet no matter what happened, Kenzie couldn't catch her breath.

"I'm going to go with them," Ainsley said quickly. "And then let Loch and Fox take me home. I'm sorry, Dare."

He held up his hand. "Not your fault. Not even a little." Loch appeared in the doorway and scowled, though Kenzie had seen the worry in his eyes when the man had come for Ainsley. "Go, before big brother gets all growly."

"Too late," Ainsley muttered. She squeezed Kenzie's hand in goodbye and left with the hulking man who, in turn, reached out and brought her close for a hug before quickly letting her go. Kenzie didn't understand the two's relationship, but as it was, she was having trouble thinking clearly with the dark spots dancing in front of her eyes.

"Shit, Kenzie?" Dare cupped her face, and she blinked rapidly. "Let's get you upstairs. You look ready to pass out."

She pulled away from him for the second time that day and blew out a breath. "I'm fine. Really. I'm just going to go to my room. Thank you."

He studied her face for a moment before taking a step away from her. She didn't know if she was pleased or not that he was giving her space. "I'll watch you walk up, just in case."

"You have a bar to run," she argued.

"And it can run itself for a minute. Come on." And with that, she followed him to the staircase and left him at the bottom as she walked to her room, her hands subtly shaking. She hated that she reacted this way to raised voices, but with the fight added to what had happened with Jeremy earlier, her nerves were shot.

She forced herself not to look at Dare when she made it to the top of the stairs and turned to her room. She wasn't sure what she'd say if she saw his face anyway.

As it was, she knew as she locked her door behind her and leaned against the solid wood, that his face would haunt her dreams again tonight.

And there was nothing she could do about it.

7

DARE LEANED BACK against the shower stall and gripped his length in his palm. He had to be quick since he was already running late, but his damn cock had been hard all day. So hard, in fact, he was pretty sure he had zipper marks on his flesh that would never go away.

Water slid down his stomach and over his hand as he cupped his balls and rocked into his hold. He only had one person on his mind as he stroked himself, and it was the one woman he knew he shouldn't.

But he couldn't help but imagine Kenzie's lips around his cock as he slid in and out of her mouth. He'd wrap that long hair of hers around his fist and get right to the edge of coming before pulling out and picking her up by her hips. Then he'd thrust into her wet heat, pounding into her as she fucked him back, hard, and they would come together in the cooling water of the shower.

His hand tightened around himself as he thought of her bright eyes going dark with lust, and soon, he was coming, leaving a trail in the water at his feet as it swirled down the drain.

"Fuck," he muttered. He was a damn fool. He quickly washed the rest of himself in the last of his warm water and turned off the shower. With a sigh, he opened the glass door and grabbed his towel so he could dry off.

He'd had a long morning at the bar dealing with his usual paperwork. And because his mind had been on Kenzie and her reaction to not only her brother but also the altercation the night before, he'd been slow. Now, he was running late for his family dinner, and he was going to hear about it.

It was bad enough that this wasn't his weekend with Nate so his mom would make pointed remarks about how she wished her grandson were there with her granddaughter. He knew she didn't mean anything by it other than professing a profound sadness that she didn't have as much time with Nate as she would like, but it still grated on Dare that he hadn't been able to be a better man in the first place. If he'd paid more attention to Monica and spent less time at his job, he might have had a fighting chance of getting more time with Nate in the end. But now there was nothing he could do, even though he'd tried to get more time a month through his lawyer.

That meant he'd sit through this meal with a family that loved him but wasn't complete because he'd made too many mistakes.

And one more issue was thinking about Kenzie the way he had. He needed to stop doing that, or he'd fuck up even more than he already had. She'd pulled away from his touch more than once even though he'd been casual about it, and that meant he shouldn't think of her in any way that was sexual.

His shower with her as his fantasy would be the last time. It had to be.

Determined to put the temptation of her out of his mind, he quickly dressed, ran a comb through his short hair, and grabbed his things so he could head to his parents'. He could have probably jogged over, but the weatherman had called for rain, so Dare drove the few minutes to the place where he'd grown up and his parents still lived.

He'd loved this house when he was a kid, and loved it even more now. It had a wide porch and tall trees and was big enough for a growing family of three rambunctious boys and a sweet-as-can-be little girl. He knew his parents wanted it filled with more grandchildren soon, and he had a feeling that Tabby and Alex would help them out with that—even all the way from Denver.

Before he could even walk up the steps, his mother opened the door, a hesitant smile on her face. "Dare. You came."

And now he felt like a heel. He'd kept his distance at first because he was trying to cope with the change—something he'd never been very good at—and then he'd been busy with work and Nate. He'd been hurt, yes, that his parents had kept their plans to themselves, but when he'd taken a step back and thought about it, he knew it was because they wanted to make sure none of their children had to worry about the details. All of them still worried, of course, but he wouldn't tell his parents that.

As the days had passed since their announcement, however, and Dare calmed down, he hadn't known how to broach the subject. So he'd avoided it and them and buried himself in work—and dreams of Kenzie.

Not that the latter meant anything. It was something he would never repeat, but he couldn't quite bury that under the rug now, could he? Not with what he'd just done in the shower less than twenty minutes ago.

But that didn't matter now. His mother was waiting for him to say something, and he hated that her smile had been hesitant because of him. Dare needed to fix this, and the only way he could think to do that was by walking right up to her and bringing her in for a hug.

She smelled of roast and a little pine, probably from what she'd been cooking and cleaning before he made it to the house. He tucked her close, and she let out a surprised sigh before wrapping her arms around his waist and tightening her hold.

"Missed you, Mom." Despite how they all sucked at communication, his family was too close for little things to keep them apart, and Dare just needed to get over himself.

She patted his back and kept her hold on him. "I missed you, too. I'm sorry, baby."

He shook his head as he pulled away so he could look at her face. "Don't apologize. It's all behind us now. You'll have time for yourself and Dad, and Kenzie is doing a bang-up job on the inn. You just surprised me, is all. Everything's fine."

His mom went up on her toes to pat his face like he was a little kid instead of her bearded adult son. "Good. Now get inside. You're late, and I'm starving."

He couldn't help but chuckle as he followed his mother inside. Fox stood next to the kitchen island with a beer in his hand, laughing at something his father said. Loch had Misty on his back and was feeding her from the antipasti plate as she bounced and giggled.

This was his family, at least part of it. Soon, they'd be off in Denver to visit Tabby and Alex for the wedding, and everyone would be together. Everyone tried to make family dinners once a month, and usually, Loch brought Ainsley with him. She was family even though she and Loch had never dated.

"I'm sorry Ainsley couldn't come," his mother said, echoing

Dare's thoughts. She was strange that way, and he was pretty sure she could read minds like she'd claimed she could when he was a kid. It was a Mom thing, apparently.

"She's grading," Misty pouted before looking over at her grandmother and fluttering her eyelashes. "I got a gold star." Dare's niece beamed, and he grinned, taking the offered beer from Fox, who had come to stand next to him.

"She'll come next time," Loch said simply and knelt down so Misty could hop off his back. "Go say hi to your uncle, bug."

"Uncle Bug!" Misty said with a laugh as she crashed into Dare's legs.

Dare rolled his eyes as Fox took a photo, grinning. Fox was always capturing their memories, though Dare wasn't sure if it was for their shared cloud album this time or just because Fox liked the name *Uncle Bug* and wanted to remember it.

"You're the bug, little bug." Dare picked up Misty and tossed her over his shoulder, and she let out a high-pitched squeal.

"Don't drop her, Uncle Bug," Fox said, laughing.

He was going to have to hit Fox later when his parents weren't looking.

"Stop roughhousing with your niece," his mom scolded. "You're teaching her bad manners."

"Tabby tackled her brothers as much as they did each other," his father put in. He held up his hands when his wife gave him a pointed look. "Or maybe just do the wrestling outside?" His parents' relationship was one Dare had wanted with someone when he'd thought about getting married, but he wasn't sure he'd ever have that. Not with whom he was as a person now.

Putting those weird thoughts from his mind, Dare laughed

and set Misty on her feet. She hugged his legs once more and then went to hug Fox's before going back to her dad's and jumping into his lap. Loch had taken a seat at the big table and let out a strangled groan when Misty jumped.

Yeah, Dare had been there with Nate's knees, as well. Kids were rough, but hell, he loved his damn family so much. One day, if Monica gave in and the courts allowed it, he'd be able to have more of this with his son. It wouldn't be stolen weekends and hesitant promises.

"Okay, come help me get all this food on the table and let's eat," his mom began. "We have lasagna, Alfredo, salad, antipasti, and tons of bread. Plus I made those mushroom things you like, Dare."

His stomach rumbled, and he took a quick sip of his beer before setting it down at his place at the table before going to help his mom. Both of his parents could cook and, thankfully, had shared their talents with all four of their kids. He was probably the last on the rankings in terms of cooking, but he did okay for himself, and Nate never went hungry the weekends Dare had him.

Dare sat by Fox, who kept trying to steal his bread even with his attention on his phone and not the conversation. His mother had tried to keep electronics away from the dinner table, but with Dare being on call at all hours of the day at the bar and restaurant, Loch the same for his business, and Fox needing to be kept up-to-date on local and national news, it just didn't make sense.

When they were all in Denver for Tabby's wedding, they'd either implode or relax. Which, he honestly didn't know.

They dug in with gusto, catching up on each other's days

and laughing like they hadn't seen each other in weeks rather than a few hours in some cases. It was times like these that Dare really missed his younger sister, and while he was happy that she'd found her fiancé and his family so she wasn't alone, it just wasn't the same without her. Sure, she called in every other day and was constantly in a texting loop with at least two of them at a time, but she was going to be a Montgomery now, and that was still a little weird for him.

His phone buzzed right when they were working on dessert—a custard his mother had made from freaking scratch that, therefore, put her on a pedestal for the night. He looked down at the screen and frowned.

"Who is it?" Loch asked softly as the other members of his family talked amongst themselves. Loch wouldn't have even asked if Dare hadn't been frowning since his big brother usually kept out of his business, and Dare tried to do the same for him.

No need to lie since his brother knew about his past. "Jesse."

"Shit." A pause. "You going to answer?"

He hadn't the past three times because he'd been a coward, but he wasn't sure he could hide for much longer. It wasn't that he never talked to her, but sometimes, his brain just couldn't function and get the words out when it came to his partner's widow.

Dare nodded as he stood up from the table and answered the phone. "One sec," he said quickly into the phone so he could get out of earshot of his family. Once he was out on the back deck, he sighed. "Sorry, Jesse."

He didn't know what he was apologizing for. For making her wait those few short moments? Not answering her calls? Pushing her away when he should have stood by her? Walking away when she'd been the one to push him out of her life first?

Or, really, was it that he was sorry that her husband was dead and he was still here, breathing?

"You answered," she said softly, her slight Columbian accent a bare whisper.

"I should have before this." He rubbed his temple and leaned against one of the pillars on the deck.

"I know you couldn't. I didn't answer every call you made when it first happened. Sometimes, we can't talk, Dare, and I understand that. It's hard and brings up memories that might be better left buried, but every time I look into my little girl's face, I can't hide from what I lost. So I'm going to keep calling, even if you don't answer. I know you'll call back when you can."

Shame crawled into his belly like a familiar, icy companion. "How's Bethany?"

He listened to her talk about her daughter, who had never gotten to know her father, and nodded along as Jesse spoke about her life. And when he hung up, he let out a breath, his hands shaking. Instead of going back inside to the warm house and laughter, he texted Loch, letting him know he was heading out, and walked around the house to his car. His brothers would let the others know why he needed to leave without saying goodbye, and they would understand.

But for now, Dare just needed a moment to catch his breath, and he wasn't sure he could do that with his family looking on.

Once again, he was running from his problems, but at least he was thinking about them this time instead of burying them so deeply that he knew they'd rot away, leaving him nothing but a husk of the man he used to be.

Instead of going home where he'd drink a beer and just sit

there wallowing, he drove to the bar. It wasn't a busy night, thankfully, and Rick and Claire had the place handled so he went back to his office and decided to get some paperwork done. He didn't want to be alone in his home without his kid and with all his memories, but he also didn't care to deal with strangers or his staff.

"Dare?"

He looked up from his desk at the sound of Kenzie's voice, surprised that she was still downstairs. "What's wrong?"

She frowned at him before walking fully into his office and closing the door behind her. "Nothing's wrong with me...why is that your first question?"

He shook his head, leaning back in his chair. "Habit, I guess. I was a cop for too long, and now I'm a bartender. It's what I do."

Kenzie studied his face before leaning against the desk. "I tend to look at the world that way, too, I guess."

He frowned and leaned back in his chair, gesturing toward the other chair in the office. "Want to sit?"

"I've been sitting most of the day going over paperwork and scheduling while I let Samantha work the front."

He remembered that Samantha was the assistant his parents had finally hired a couple of days ago. And since the other woman was in training, he bet that Kenzie hadn't left the other woman on her own much.

She shrugged when he mentioned it. "True. She's smart and learns quickly, but while I didn't want to hover, neither of us is ready for her to take over all the responsibilities completely."

"You jumped right in far quicker," he pointed out.

Kenzie smiled softly. "I had more experience, and your parents didn't cut the strings completely. They're still around."

"True, but not as much, and I'm grateful for that."

She snorted. "Like that your family isn't in your business as much as they were?"

"I don't mind that even when I think I do." He let out a short laugh. "I meant the fact that my parents are actually sleeping in most days and using the word *vacation*. It's been far too long, you know?"

At that, she smiled, and his breath caught. He'd known she was beautiful, couldn't help but realize it. But when she smiled, and the darkness slid from her gaze? Fucking stunning.

But the thought of that darkness reminded him of the fight in the bar. "Did the fight bother you?"

Her face shut down, going back to that iciness he'd first seen, the coldness he'd thought had melted away. "Fight?"

He was messing this up, and he didn't know why, but he couldn't stop now, not when he wanted to know more about her even though he shouldn't. Instead of listening to his inner voice that told him to stop the conversation, he stood and moved toward her so he hovered over her, a mere breath away.

"You know what I'm talking about. Those guys at the bar who were out of line and drunk off their asses. You froze up and looked like you wanted to be anywhere but there. I wish I could have gotten them out of the place sooner, and I'm sorry if it hurt you. Or brought up memories you'd rather forget."

"I'm fine, Dare." She met his eyes before looking away, her face expressionless. "Things aren't always as they seem. I'm fine now. I wasn't always. But like you, I've moved on."

He cursed under his breath, and she stiffened. Instead of doing what he should, what they *both* should, he cupped her face with his palm and brought her gaze to his.

"I'm still sorry it upset you. I don't like when you're not yourself. Or at least, not like the woman I've come to know."

She blinked up at him and licked her lips, bringing his attention to the curve of her mouth. He wasn't even sure she was aware she'd done it.

"I'm not upset anymore."

He inhaled her scent, trying to calm himself, but his heart still raced. "Can I kiss you?"

He didn't know why he'd asked, other than the fact that he truly wanted to taste her. With anyone else, he would have just kissed them, knowing they wanted it from their body language and the look in their eyes. He wouldn't have had to ask. Kenzie? He couldn't read her, even though he thought he might be able to one day. So he'd asked. He'd bared himself to her and asked.

She didn't startle, didn't blink. "You want to kiss me?"

"Yes," he said patiently. "I want to kiss you."

"We shouldn't."

It wasn't a no, but he still didn't move. "No, we probably shouldn't. But I still want to. Will you let me?"

She swallowed hard, and he could feel her jaw work as she did so. "I...we can't...okay."

He was the one who blinked this time. "Okay?"

"Okay...if you still want to."

He chuckled. "We sound like we're in middle school now, trying to figure out how to kiss."

She smiled again, and before she could say anything, he lowered his head and took her lips with his. She gasped into his mouth, but he didn't deepen the kiss, not yet. He knew he needed to take his time with her, to take his time for both of them.

She tasted like coffee and sweetness, an intoxicating combination that set him on edge. When she hesitantly placed her hands on his sides, he groaned, but still didn't kiss her harder. Instead, he tasted her mouth, explored her feel, and made sure this kiss would be ingrained on his mind—and hopefully hers— forever.

And when he pulled back, they were both breathless.

"I need to go," she whispered. "I can't think."

He swallowed hard, resting his forehead on hers. "I can never think when you're around."

When she let out a strained laugh, he pulled back to look at her.

"You have to stop saying things like that. We don't like each other, remember? We're keeping our distance."

He tucked a piece of her hair behind her ear. "I don't think we were ever enemies, Kenzie. That was just a lie we told ourselves so we wouldn't do what we just did."

"I should go." She pulled away from him, and he let his hands drop to his sides. "I…" She didn't say anything else; instead, she walked out of his office, leaving him alone with his thoughts and his hope that he hadn't just messed things up royally.

He hadn't meant to kiss her, hadn't meant to ask.

But now that he had? Well, hell, he wasn't sure he'd had enough of her.

Not even close.

8

KENZIE'S NEW GOAL in life was not to make as many mistakes as she had in her past but with that kiss the previous night with Dare...well, she wasn't quite sure she'd accomplished that. What on earth had she been thinking letting Dare kiss her like that? What had she been thinking kissing him back?

She *hadn't* been thinking, that was the only answer.

She'd already told herself that she had to stay away from Dare Collins. He was her boss's son, first off. Secondly, he worked pretty much two full-time jobs and probably as many hours as she did—if not more—meaning, they'd never see each other *except* at work. It was also clear that he had as many issues in his past that he hadn't worked through as she did. She might not know what had happened to make him leave the police force or why his eyes grew dark whenever anyone mentioned it in passing, but she knew when a man held secrets.

Mysteries that were not hers to know for damn good reason.

Dare also had a son, one whom he did didn't see often enough for his liking. She'd seen the way his eyes lit up at the sight of Nathan, and it killed her that she couldn't do anything about it for him. His ex had full custody, and while it looked like Dare was a good father, he clearly didn't get many hours with his little boy.

She didn't know the whys of that, but she had a feeling all his hurts were connected, and because she had enough of that on her own, she *knew* she couldn't risk adding any more to either of them.

"Miss?"

Kenzie pulled herself out of the dangerous labyrinth that was her thoughts when it came to Dare and smiled at Mrs. Roberts, one of her guests for the next two evenings.

"Hello, Mrs. Roberts, what can I do for you?"

The older woman smiled at Kenzie and patted her hair self-consciously. "Um…we seem to have…well, we have an issue in our bathroom." When she blushed, Kenzie had a feeling it was a clogged toilet. If she couldn't handle it, then she'd have to call Loch since he seemed to know a little bit of everything, including plumbing, but hopefully, Kenzie could do it on her own.

"I see. I'm sorry about that. Let me go up with you and see what I can do."

If possible, Mrs. Roberts blushed harder. "You see…um…well…the toilet is clogged," she whispered.

"I understand. I'll be happy to take care of it." Poor woman. She could understand how embarrassing it could be in a public place even though it was a normal occurrence in the grand scheme of things.

"You don't understand," she whispered, looking over her shoulder as if someone could overhear. There was no one in the hallway, and voices didn't carry that well with all the furnishings and wallpaper. "It's not clogged with the usual, well, you know."

Kenzie did her best to keep her face neutral. "Oh?"

The woman in her sixties spoke quickly at this point. "Mr.

Roberts and I are here on our anniversary. We wanted to spice things up, you see, and it turns out neither of us is particularly fond of the edible panties we brought. Not the best flavor, though the reviews said otherwise. Since there was so much left of it, we thought we'd flush the remaining parts down the toilet instead of leaving it in the trash for the maid or you to find. I'm so sorry."

Kenzie did not laugh. She didn't even smile; instead, she nodded and did her best to keep the images of the older couple using edible underwear out of her mind.

Only there really wasn't any hope of that, was there?

Well, it wasn't the most embarrassing story she'd heard in her life while in hotel and inn management, but it might be up there on the list.

"You know what? Why don't you and Mr. Roberts go out for dinner like you'd planned to this evening? I know you have tickets for the theatre we have in town, and you wouldn't want to waste them. While you're gone, we'll take care of your room for you so when you get back, you won't have to worry about it."

Mrs. Roberts nodded, relief clear on her face. "Thank you so much. Oh, just thank you."

"No worries. It's what I'm here for."

And when the couple left, Mr. Roberts not meeting Kenzie's gaze, she let out a breath and went to find her plunger. This was the life she'd signed up for, after all—the non-glamorous parts and all.

"THANKS FOR HELPING," Kenzie said two hours later as she sipped whiskey at the bar next to Ainsley. "Apparently, that was a two-person job."

Her new friend shuddered before taking a sip from one of the three glasses on their shared flight. It had become their thing to try out different whiskeys and mixed drinks with the namesake liquor, and thankfully, they made mini-flights for those who didn't want to end up stumbling their way to their rooms. It was also Whiskey Wednesday at the bar and on social media, so everything was half price. That was a win in her opinion.

"Thank you for not only letting me shower after that, but for lending me your clothes." Ainsley picked at the sleeve of the billowy tunic Kenzie loved and grinned. "I might need to steal this."

Kenzie narrowed her eyes, though her lips twitched. "Do, and I'll hunt you down. I can run in heels, you know."

"I can only run in sensible heels, not those stilts you wear." She eyed Kenzie's legs and sighed. "It's not fair that your legs always look that good, even in your flats right now."

Kenzie looked down at her pretty black and pink flowered lacey flats and smiled. "They're my favorites." She had a thing for shoes, she couldn't help it.

"If only you weren't a half size smaller than me," Ainsley said with longing.

"I have a feeling I'm going to have to lock up my closet." She grinned as she said it. She'd never had a friend who she could share clothes with before or ask for help in unclogging a toilet full of edible underwear.

That was true friendship right there.

"I'm glad we got the mini-flight because I need to go home and work a bit. I probably shouldn't even be having these three tiny sips I'm having all on a school night, but after what we just did? It's bottom's up."

"Sips up," Kenzie corrected, frowned. "Or just sips? I'm really not good at this whole talking thing, and I've only had two sips."

"Next time, we'll just share a whiskey sour and call it a night," the other woman said on a laugh. "And with that, I should really go. I swear the stack of papers gets bigger each time I look at it."

"My desk looks the same, mostly likely." And though they were both complaining, she knew, like her, Ainsley loved her job and wouldn't trade it for the world. Though she would probably say goodbye to grading if she could.

Since they were almost done with their drinks as it was, she downed the last of the one she liked the most and paid her bill before going back upstairs to see if there was anything else she could do before she called it a night.

And if she were being truthful with herself, she was doing her best to avoid seeing Dare before he showed up like he usually did in the evenings when he didn't work. The man was more of a workaholic than she was, and that was saying something. She didn't know what she was going to say to him, nor what she *could* say the next time she saw him.

So avoidance seemed like the best answer.

And the weakest, but she never claimed to be strong.

She'd just gotten to her desk when her phone buzzed. Since she'd had a little whiskey and was thinking about Dare and too in her head, she answered without looking at the screen.

"Kenzie. It's about time you answered my phone call. You've always been useless, but at least once you did what you should and answered the damn phone."

David. How could she have been so *stupid*? She hadn't heard his voice since the divorce and always archived his messages for her lawyer without listening. Why hear him when his voice haunted her dreams?

She didn't say a word, she just hung up, her hands shaking and her palms damp. She knew he'd call again and yell into her voicemail.

"Kenzie? What's wrong?"

Dare had her in his arms before she could protest or even get her thoughts in order. And as much as she wanted to pull away and find her balance on her own, she couldn't. Instead, she leaned into him, taking his comfort and strength and hating herself just that much more for it.

He slid his hands through her hair and held her close, and she did her best not to break down into tears. Thankfully, her eyes didn't sting because she'd told herself that she was done crying over David's words and threats. He meant *nothing* to her.

Okay, that was a lie, but she refused to let her ex-husband's hate control her actions and dictate her emotions anymore.

"Kenzie?" Dare's beard rubbed the top of her head as he held her close, and she closed her eyes, relishing his hold, his touch, even though she told herself she shouldn't.

"I'm fine," she lied, her eyes still closed.

Dare didn't say anything, but she could hear the disappointment in his drawn-out breath. She didn't know why she felt such a connection to this man. And she could still taste him on her lips though she'd done her best to forget it.

And she was letting him hold her, something she'd never thought she would let another man do.

"It was my ex-husband," she said after a moment, her voice almost wooden.

Dare's hands froze on the back of her head before he started petting her again as if he were trying to make everything better with just a simple caress. But nothing was that simple.

Finally, Kenzie pulled back so she could collect her thoughts and get her words out. "David and I have been divorced for almost a year now, but he doesn't seem to understand that divorce means I don't want to talk to him. Ever."

Dare's jaw tightened, but he didn't say anything, as if he knew she needed time to say what she had to before she could respond to any of his questions.

"I met David when I was nineteen. He was a few years older than me, but I didn't care at the time. I thought I knew what I was doing. He was so charming, so caring. He was a big player in a major company and eventually became the CFO. In fact, he still is. He's powerful and knows it."

"Kenzie…"

She shook her head, needing to get it out. "I didn't realize he was controlling everything I did until it was too late." She paused. "I could have said *almost* too late, but in reality, it was too late for me to go back to the Kenzie I was before I met him. I'll never be that person again."

"Did he hurt you?" Dare growled out, his voice low. "Did he fucking touch you?"

She met his eyes, raising her chin like she always did when she was facing her fears these days. "Just once. He hit me once, and I left. Or I tried to. It took me a while to get out and figure out how to be me without being his wife. But abuse doesn't have to be with fists." She pressed her lips together, collecting herself once more. She'd said the words, and there was no going back.

"What did he do, Kenzie? You can tell me, unless you want

to stop and go have coffee and talk about nothing important. Don't share with me because you think I need you to. Do it because you want to."

And that right there was why she was going to tell him about her past. The more she kept it bottled up inside, the more she hid it from her present, the more *important* it became. Her path was not defined by a single instant. Her way in life was not delineated by her marriage. She was not defined by *him*. By David.

Her life was hers—hers to live, hers to thrive within.

And that was why she wanted Dare to know her. Because it was her choice, not a set of circumstances.

"I married David six months after I met him. I never once believed he was my Prince Charming—I don't believe in fairy tales. But I thought he was my happily ever after, knowing that with that comes work. Everything started out okay as those things usually do."

"There's nothing usual about what you're telling me," Dare said softly. "There's nothing normal about abuse."

Again, she could see how he'd been a cop before this. He'd seen more than she could ever dream—not that he'd told her anything about his time then. But they weren't together, were they? They didn't know each other beyond what they were slowly learning. Why was she telling him this? Why did she *need* to? They'd kissed, they'd touched, and they had a connection, though she wasn't sure what it all meant. And because *something* inside was telling her to tell him, she continued.

"He slowly changed the way I worked, made sure I was home more often for him. He belittled me. Told me I was fat or ugly or not caring enough. He said I never lived up to his needs. But he never truly yelled at first or made it seem like he was doing any of that. It was all the little things that added up to the bigger ones." She met his gaze and tried to catch her breath. "I know others had worse. *Have* worse."

"Stop." He reached out slowly to cup her face, and she didn't pull away from him. Progress. "Don't compare your pain to others. It's *your* pain. It matters."

She swallowed hard. "I hated myself for what I let him do to me. I quit hanging out with my friends." She didn't have any left by the time she left the city. "I quit being me. But I'm working on that. I've *been* working on it. I might still jump at loud noises or freak out in a bar when two big men start to fight, but I don't break down like I would have before. I've come a long way."

Dare brushed her cheek with his thumb, and it took all within her not to move into his touch. "Hell yeah, you have." He paused. "He called you today." Not a question since she'd already told him, but it brought her back to the present rather than wading through her past.

She turned from Dare, the numbness from before replaced by anger. "He's been calling since the divorce. I usually ignore him, but I wasn't looking when I answered today. My mind was on so many things." *On you*, she thought, but she didn't say that.

His eyes narrowed as if something she'd said clicked. "He was the one who called you during your first lunch here in the bar."

She'd almost forgotten. Not because it hadn't meant something to her, but because David called so often, it was hard to focus on each and every occurrence. But she *did* vividly remember the way Dare had come over to make sure she was okay. She'd been so wrong about him. So, so wrong.

"I keep the voicemails for my lawyer, but that's all I can do."

"And you don't have a damn retraining order?" He roughly ran his hand through his hair but didn't move toward her.

She shook her head, clenching her fists in front of her. "He never leaves messages that could be used against him. He only yells and threatens me when it's not recorded. He's never let the world see who he truly is, and because of that, the system doesn't work for me." She shrugged, but she was anything but casual about her words.

"I was part of the system. And I know for a fact that it fails more than it should. But, hell, Kenzie, I'm so damn sorry."

"I'm better. I promise. I'm not the same woman who married him. I'm also not the same person who finally left him," she said honestly. She couldn't have Dare see her as weak. She didn't want to be a frail imitation of the woman she could be. "I'm better," she repeated.

Dare studied her face. "I believe that, Red. You're damn strong if you can stand here and even tell me any of this. You shouldn't have been forced to go through what you did, and you damn sure shouldn't have to feel like you need to tell me anything more if you don't want to. You don't owe me anything, but the fact that you opened up? That you trusted me? That means a whole hell of a lot." He paused, a frown marring his face. "And your brother? You said you were cut off from everything, but I met your brother."

This time, she was the one who frowned. "He's still friends with David."

"Are you fucking kidding me?"

She shook her head and was grateful when Dare moved just a little closer. He wasn't afraid to be near her, and that wasn't fear running through her veins at the mention of him. The dichotomy of her past and present had never been so vivid.

"Jeremy…" She sighed. "He's my baby brother." When Dare didn't say anything, she continued. "My parents, when they were alive, coddled him. So did I. I know we did. But he was my baby brother," she repeated. "And though my parents and I loved him, he grew up into a man I don't recognize. He feels like the world owes him for merely breathing. He wants to be David. Wants the money and the power and resents the fact that I severed Jeremy's direct connection to David."

"Jesus Christ."

It was her turn to snort. "Pretty much. What you saw in this office was the first time he's laid his hands on me." She raised her chin. "And the *last* time. I'm no longer in contact with either of them if I can help it. I'm not who I used to be, and I don't want to be dragged back into a past I'd rather forget because they don't seem to understand." She ran her hands through her hair and let out a rough laugh. "And I have no idea why I told you all of that. I've only told my therapist. Hell, I haven't even told Ainsley and I've talked to her more than I have you since I moved here."

This time when Dare moved toward her, he didn't hesitate to run his hand through her hair. "I'm glad you told me. That you trust me." He leaned forward, resting his forehead on hers. "I know it wasn't easy, and I want to go and beat the shit out of both of the men in your life, guys that should have protected you, but I won't. I'm so fucking sorry you went through that, but you have to know that you're so damn strong for standing here and telling me. For *living*. You laugh with your friends. You're making new connections every day that you work here and meet new people in Whiskey. You're not hiding. You're *thriving*. I don't know how you do it."

She met his gaze and licked her lips. "One day at a time. It's the only thing I can tell myself."

He leaned back and traced her jaw with his fingertip, sending shivers down her spine. "One day at a time," he repeated.

"Will you kiss me?" she blurted, surprising both of them. "I mean…"

He blinked. "That's not where I thought this conversation was going."

"I know, but I don't want to talk about the past anymore. I don't want to live in it. I want to worry about the future and the *now*. So, will you kiss me? Will you help me just be?" She couldn't believe she was asking that of him and yet she knew it was what she needed. She might not know what was coming next, and this was probably a mistake, but it was *her* mistake to make.

In answer, he leaned down and took her lips.

Thank. God.

He licked and sucked on her mouth, making her ache, and forcing her to press her legs together to relieve the tension. Because she didn't want anyone else to barge in on them, they both stopped kissing long enough to for her to lead them both to her small apartment. They were both breathless by the time she got her key in the lock and the door closed behind them but Kenzie didn't want to let her brain think too hard about what she was about to do. If she did, he might pull away, mistake or no.

"What do you like?" he whispered against her mouth, pulling her closer with his hands on her butt. His rigid erection pressed into her stomach, and he bent down so he could run his teeth lightly over her ear.

"You." She moaned, leaning her head back. "Just…just don't hold my arms too tightly. Anything else is what I want. Anything."

She knew he was swallowing back the rage at *why* she didn't want him to hold her arms too tightly. "That I can do." Then there weren't that many words spoken between them; there didn't need to be.

He pulled her into her bedroom, and soon, her legs were pressed firmly against the bed as he let his lips trail down her neck, sucking and licking, sending her so close to the edge with only his mouth on her skin that she knew once they had their clothes off she'd combust.

He lowered his head and kissed the top of her breast through her shirt, and she squirmed in his hold. Needing more contact, she pulled away and slowly undid the buttons on her blouse. Though her hands shook, she kept her eyes on his, needing him to know that she was in this *with* him and not running away scared.

She would never be afraid again.

His gaze lowered to her hands when she finished undoing her blouse, letting the fabric drop to the floor. When he looked at her lace-covered breasts, he swallowed hard, licking his lips. Then he had his shirt over his head and his mouth on her neck again. Damn it, she loved when he kissed her neck, and from what she could tell, he loved it just as much.

When he kissed her breast again, this time over the lace covering her nipple, she let out a shocked moan.

"Your tits are so fucking sexy, Red. I would fuck them right now if I didn't know that I'd blow right then. I need to be inside you instead.

She shivered. "You want to fuck my boobs? I thought guys only did that in porn."

His big hand cupped the back of her head, tangling her hair in his fingers. "I'll show you exactly what I like. And your tits? They're up there." He slid his hand up her skirt, his fingers caressing her skin forcing tiny gasps from her mouth. Then he palmed her ass, his finger sliding under her thong and between her crack. "But your ass? Yeah, I think I might dig your ass even more."

"Then you're going to have to see me naked to be sure." He grinned wickedly at her.

"Yeah?"

"Of course, I have to see all of you, as well. For comparisons."

"Then I guess we should get naked because I'm going to need to lick that pussy of yours. Now."

She was on her back in seconds, her legs over his shoulders as he rucked up her skirt and breathed hot hair over her panties. Before she could protest—not that she was planning to really—he had her thong shoved to the side and his mouth on her pussy.

Dear. Lord.

He ate her out like a starving man finding a feast. His tongue and fingers worked in tandem, bringing her close to the edge before backing away just when she was ready to crest. The scrape of his beard along her inner thighs made her even wetter, and she knew her skin was damp all over. *All. Over.*

Then he growled against her clit, and she came, her body shaking and his fingers sliding in and out of her in a punishing thrust. She clamped down around him, sending a groan out of his lips and against her clit. That just made her come harder.

When he stood up, his lips were wet with her arousal, and he grinned. "You taste like honey."

"Really?" she asked, spreading herself wider so he could stand between her legs.

In answer, he took his finger and wiped her juices from his mouth then rubbed his fingertip over her lips. Her tongue darted out, and she moaned.

"Sweet."

"I'm going to fuck you hard into the mattress, Kenzie. You think I'm going too rough or not letting you move? You tell me. Got me?"

She nodded and reached around to undo her bra. Her breasts felt heavy, aching. Her nipples were hard little points, and as Dare undid his pants and pushed them down over his hips, she pinched them, causing them both to moan as he watched her.

"Do it again," he growled, palming his cock. He was hard and thick, with a tiny drop of fluid on the end.

She rolled her nipples between her fingers and sucked in a sharp breath at the sensation.

"I need a condom. One sec." He went back to his jeans and pulled one out of his wallet, opening it and rolling it over his length in the next instant. "I wasn't planning this, and I only have the one, so we're going to make it count." He swallowed hard. "Probably should have come beforehand so I wouldn't blow my load as soon as I'm inside you."

She loved his crassness, loved the way he didn't hold back even after everything she'd told him. No, he wouldn't hold her down or take away any of her mobility, but he wouldn't treat her like some fragile flower either.

She *wasn't* a fragile flower, damn it. She wasn't made of glass. She was a real woman who had needs and who had only been able to use her hand to come in ages. Now, she had a man who'd not only gone down on her without reciprocation but also wanted to make sure that this night was good for her.

She'd take him as he came and she knew he'd damn well do the same for her.

That was why she was throwing caution to the wind and letting this happen tonight. That was why she knew she might be making a mistake, but letting it be her mistake and not someone else's.

"I need you in me," she said finally, her voice a throaty purr.

"That I can do, Red." He knelt on the bed between her legs. "I've been dreaming about having these long legs of yours wrapped around my hips as I fuck you." He gave her a cocky grin. "Of course, I've also been dreaming about you riding me so hard your breasts bounce, and I just sit back and let you do all the work so…"

She laughed and reached out to pinch his hip. She'd never thought she'd laugh during sex again. Hell, she'd never thought she'd have sex again.

And here she was, having some of the best sex of her life with her boss's son, and he hadn't even let her touch his cock yet. What a night.

"Just get in me already," she teased.

He grinned and positioned himself at her entrance. "That I can do." Then he thrust in and out in small movements, causing them both to gasp. He was so thick, so freaking big, that she was afraid she wouldn't be able to take all of him, but she was also so wet that he could slide in and out easily.

He kept his gaze on hers until he was fully inside her to the hilt. Then he closed his eyes and moaned. "You're so damn tight."

She squeezed her inner muscles, and he lowered himself to one arm, sliding the other between them as he opened his eyes. When he flicked her clit with his fingers, she sucked in a breath.

Then he *moved.*

He hovered over her, taking her lips, playing with her breasts, her clit, her hips, but never once did he hold her down or make her feel caged. Instead, she felt *cherished, needed.*

She arched into him, needing him as much as he seemed to need her. And when she came again, he picked up his pace before coming deep inside her, filling the condom in spurts.

Then he cupped her face and kissed her so sweetly, tears spilled down her cheeks. And he kissed each one of those in turn.

Kenzie had no idea what they were doing, but she knew that once they figured it out, it might all be a horrible mistake.

Yet she couldn't care. Not then. Not when he kissed away her tears and made her feel more human, more like a woman, than she ever had before.

Dare was a dangerous man—something she'd known from the first time she set eyes on him.

But it wasn't until he held her close as they both fought to catch their breaths that she caught a glimpse of how truly dangerous he was.

To her heart.

9

DARE KNEW HE was a selfish bastard and what he'd done with Kenzie the night before just cemented that fact. He couldn't get the feeling of her underneath him out of his mind. It was almost tangible, as if he could still feel her beneath him. As if he could still taste the sweetness of her on his tongue.

He'd wanted to break something when she told him about her ex-husband and brother. He'd seen some of the worst of humanity when he was a cop, yet time and again, the dregs of civilization surprised him. He hated that he could still be shocked after all this time, that he wasn't some jaded old cop who thought he'd seen it all.

He hadn't.

While he had known something was going on with Kenzie, he hadn't known how far she'd come. She was so damn strong; he was in awe of her fight, her journey. Now that he knew, it made sense why she formed that icy exterior when she felt threatened. Or how she'd raise her chin when she needed to hold herself close and gather strength.

Kenzie Owens was so much more than the parts that made up her past, and he was once again in awe of her. He wasn't worthy of the woman she'd been before or the person she was now after everything she'd been through.

Dare sat on the edge of his bed, the silence of his empty house deafening. He shouldn't have touched Kenzie. He knew that, yet he'd done it anyway. He'd told himself he would stay away, that he had no time for complications or anything that could come from being anywhere near his innkeeper, yet he hadn't listened to himself.

His hands were dirty—his past decisions had tarnished him. There was a reason he hadn't been able to get full custody of his son. There was a reason Monica had never wanted more from him other than the small connection they had. She'd taken their son and found her happiness with a man who, in her opinion, was far better than Dare, and that was something he knew he agreed with…even if he didn't want to.

Kenzie had been through hell and back, and she deserved far more than a man like him.

Yet he was just selfish enough to want more with her. He wanted to make her laugh. Wanted to see the darkness in her eyes fade away as she learned to live in the now again. Yet how could he want to see that when his own darkness filled his eyes when he thought about *why* he wasn't a cop anymore?

He swallowed hard and sat up so he could look at the open letter on his bed. It was fate's timing that the letter had arrived that day, the morning after he'd slid inside Kenzie and fought to forget the world. Life knew he wasn't the man Kenzie needed him to be and it didn't want him to forget it.

Ever.

The letter beside him proved that.

With regret, he reached out and picked up the fragile piece of paper that already had a few creases in it from his clenched fist. He shouldn't have opened the damn thing. Hell, he shouldn't even have *received* it. There was no way this person should have his mailing address, but things were different than they used to be, and keeping people safe and out of the public eye wasn't always easy.

It never was, not really.

You killed my dad. You don't deserve to be out of jail. Why do you get to walk free when my dad died? Why do you get to be okay when you killed him? If my dad killed someone, he would be in jail. But now he's dead, and you're free.

~~*I hope you die too.*~~

I hate you.

I hate you.

I hate you.

The letter wasn't signed. It didn't need to be. He knew the child, now a teenager, who had written it. He'd never met the kid, but had seen photos of him. The little boy had his father's eyes.

Eyes that held no life anymore because of choices that he and Dare and his partner had made.

Dare clenched his fist once more, the paper crackling in his hand. He'd have to save it and send it to his old department. That was procedure, and the fact that there were plans in place for this kind of thing sickened him.

It was one reason he was glad Nate wasn't here.

Being with Dare wasn't safe for his son.

It never would be.

His phone buzzed in his pocket, and he angled his hips so he could dig it out, answering when he saw the readout.

"Jesse."

"Did you get a letter, too?" she asked, her voice small. He hated that she whispered as if someone could hear, as if the letters in their hands threatened what they had.

Dare stood up quickly, anger flooding his veins at the thought of someone sending Jesse and her little girl a letter like he'd just gotten in the mail. *No one* was supposed to come at Jessie for what went on in the line of duty. No one.

"I got one," he growled out. "How did you know? What did yours say? Do you need me to come over?"

"Slow down, Dare. I'm safe. Bethany is upstairs playing and doesn't know anything is wrong." A pause. "And nothing *is* wrong, Dare. Nothing is going to happen. That child is hurting because he misses his father and he's taking it out on you and wants to take it out on Jason. But since Jason isn't here anymore, he sent the letter to me. I only know you got one too because my letter mentions yours."

"I'll come by and pick it up and take it to the precinct." He didn't want her to have to go into the place where Jason had worked, had laughed, and had spent his last hours before he died.

"I'll come by tonight for dinner and bring Bethany. How's that?" She didn't say anything else, and he kicked himself for putting that uncertainty in her voice.

"Will six work?" he asked. It was four now, and he had to work that night anyway.

"Six is just fine. It will be good to see you."

There was a wealth of meaning in those words, and when he hung up, he knew that after tonight, things would have to change. He hoped to hell they changed for the better, though.

THE BAR WAS busy enough when he walked in and went through the day's issues. Claire had the restaurant just about ready to open for the evening, and they had decent reservations all night so he only had to go through a few things with her before heading back to the bar. He was damned lucky to have found Claire, and he had a feeling he'd be giving her a raise soon if their revenue kept up like it was.

Work was the only safe and healthy thing in his life. No, that wasn't true. His family was what kept him able to do anything and breathe. His family. His son. And his bar.

But thoughts of the letter he'd gotten in the mail kept coming back to him, reminding him that while he might have fought for what he had, he wasn't worth getting more.

"Hey, you're here," Kenzie said as she walked up to him in her prim and proper innkeeper outfit complete with high heels.

He *really* liked those shoes.

She didn't move to touch him, and he knew that was because they hadn't talked since he left her room. Neither one of them knew where they stood with one another, and the fact that his past was coming into the bar soon to meet with him just reminded him that he should back away and tell Kenzie that she wasn't for him.

But he didn't.

He couldn't.

"I'm on shift tonight," he said, coming closer to her. He didn't touch her since they were both at work and he had no idea how to walk that line, but he still wanted to be close.

"I remember." She gave him a weird look, and he sighed.

"Sorry, I have a lot on my mind tonight, but I'm really glad you're here." He licked his lips when she did, and he held back a groan at the sight.

That brought a smile to her face. "I'm glad. I planned on catching something to eat here tonight rather than cooking for myself. I've become lazy since moving here."

"We have good food. Hard to want to cook. I do the same. Want to eat at the bar?"

"That sounds like a plan. I have a few things to finish up before the night crew starts, but I saw you walk by."

"I'm glad you came over." And because he couldn't quite help himself, he reached out and tucked a stray tendril of hair behind her ear. "See you soon?"

"Soon." She turned to walk away then stopped and looked back at him. "I guess we should figure out what we're doing and if we're going to be out in public or not, right?"

He snorted, shaking his head. "Yeah. Yeah, that might have to move to the top of our list of things to talk about."

She let out a relieved breath. "Thank God." He watched her walk away before turning at the sound of a familiar voice.

"Jesse. You're here." He smiled at the beautiful woman with light brown skin and dark curls framing her face. She held the hand of a little girl with black curly hair and skin a slightly darker shade of brown. The little girl also had her father's eyes, smile, and chin.

It was a shock to the gut every time he saw the two of them, and tonight was no different.

"It's good to see you, no matter the reason," Jesse said. "Say hi to your Uncle Dare, baby girl."

"Hi," Bethany said with a smile, ducking her head.

"Hey there." He cleared his throat. He wished Nate was here, and he promised himself that the kids would get to know each other more than they did now. He'd make sure Misty knew Bethany, as well. If anyone could make someone smile, it was his niece. "In the mood for dinner?"

"We're famished. Aren't we?"

Bethany smiled then looked away from Dare, giggling.

"Okay, then. Let's head to the bar."

They were just moving away from the busier foyer when Kenzie walked down the stairs and stopped at the sight of Dare and his new companions. She gave him a weird look, and he held back a curse at what this probably looked like.

"Jessie, this is Kenzie, our new innkeeper and…well…this is Kenzie." He *used* to be articulate. "Kenzie, this is Jesse and Bethany." He kept his voice casual, hoping he wasn't complicating his world even more with a small introduction that was anything but small.

Jesse held out a hand. "Hi there. I was married to Jason." At Kenzie's blank look, Jessie continued after raising her brows at Dare. "Dare's old partner. This is our daughter, Bethany."

Understanding filled Kenzie's eyes, and she smiled, though he knew it was strained. He hadn't told her about why he left the force, and that was on him. She'd shared with him, and he hadn't done the same.

"I'm glad to meet you." She bent to be at Bethany's level. "And, hi there. It's nice to meet you, too."

Bethany ducked behind her mom's legs but waved. He'd had no idea the little girl was *this* shy. Hell, he should have known. He should have helped out more than he had and not just with money. He was such a damn idiot and too used to hiding from his problems.

That was something he needed to change.

"I know you need to work in a bit behind the bar, but how about we all get a booth and eat?" Jessie smiled between the two of them, and Dare held back a groan. She'd always been a matchmaker, and it seemed that hadn't changed a bit.

"Oh, I don't want to intrude. I was just going to eat at the bar."

Dare shook his head. "No, come eat with us. I want you to."

Kenzie looked between them and then finally at the little girl who stared up at the adults with wide eyes. "Okay, then."

IT HADN'T BEEN the most awkward dinner in history, but it hadn't been the easiest either. Since he and Kenzie hadn't talked about their relationship, he hadn't been sure how to introduce her, and it had all gone downhill from there. They'd kept polite conversation and never once brought up why Dare and Jesse didn't talk much now or why Bethany seemed so shy. But it had been the start of something, at least. What, he didn't know.

Only when Jesse had handed over her letter without a word had Kenzie given him an odd look. They'd all parted ways after dinner, and Kenzie had promised him that she'd see him after his shift. They apparently had a lot to talk about.

So now, Rick was closing with Shelly, and Dare stood outside of Kenzie's room, his hands fisted at his sides, and his belly aching.

He had to tell her about Jesse, about why he was no longer a cop, and why they needed to stop doing whatever they were doing. Only he had a feeling he wouldn't get to the last part. After all, he was a selfish bastard.

Finally, he knocked once, and Kenzie opened the door immediately.

"I thought you'd stand out here forever." At his raised brow, she pointed at the floor beneath his feet. "I heard the boards creak beneath your feet." She frowned. "I'll add that to the list for Loch."

"He'd probably enjoy it," he said dryly. His brother weird, after all. But Dare was weirder. He studied her face, searching for what, he didn't know. "Can I come in?"

She stepped back without a word, and he followed her into the small apartment. It was the only room upstairs that had its own kitchen and living area. It had been for previous innkeepers over the years even though his parents had never actually lived here. Kenzie had added her own special touches to the place since she moved in, things he'd missed the night before when he'd been buried deep inside her.

He pushed those thoughts from his mind, doing his best not to shift from leg to leg and adjust himself. They were here to talk about what they were going to do about last night, and for him to tell her more about why he'd had dinner with Jesse and Bethany. He wasn't here to let his cock do the thinking.

"So…" Kenzie said, blowing out a breath. "I'm really not good at this, you know. Before David, I only had one other boyfriend, and that was in high school. So figuring out what to do the morning—or day, rather—after sleeping with someone is so far out of my wheelhouse it's not funny."

"You're not the only one," he muttered. "I honestly have no idea what I'm doing here, Red. And I feel like every move I make is the wrong one, you know? That I keep fucking up."

"So we're on the same page with that at least," she said with a wry grin. "We probably should have talked *before* we slept together, huh?"

He reached out and cupped her cheek, unable to hold back from touching her any longer. "I was thinking I should have taken you on a date at least."

"We're going about this all backwards. The thing is, I don't even know what *this* is."

He lowered his head, taking her lips in a gentle touch before pulling back. "I don't know either, except we should probably stop."

She met his gaze. "Because I work for your parents and things could get complicated."

"And neither of us is looking for something serious, so we should make sure we don't mess things up more than we already have."

"I agree." She paused. "But we're still touching each other."

He pulled away, pacing back and forth. "I can't seem to stop wanting to touch you, Kenzie. And I *know* it's bad for both of us."

"So what if we do our best not to make it matter?" He turned and frowned. "I mean, making the seriousness of it not matter. Not us personally. I honestly have no idea what I'm saying." She threw her hands up in the air and started pacing like he had been. "I'm not ready for anything serious. You said that, and we both know it's true. But I'm tired of living my life being so afraid of trying anything new that I miss everything in the process."

"So you want to sleep with me again?" he asked, his dick on alert.

She blushed but kept her eyes on his. It was damn sexy. "Yes. And from the way your cock is straining your jeans, I'm not the only one."

"I'm going to take you out then, Kenzie. I'm not going to hide whatever this is because it might be easier. I don't want secrets."

"I don't want secrets either." She met his gaze again, and he knew he had to tell her more about his past.

"Before we do anything else, though, I should tell you more about Jesse…and Jason."

"You don't have to, Dare. If it's too hard, you truly don't need to bare your soul. We just said this wouldn't be serious."

"I can't be the man who gets to touch you without telling you why I shouldn't be that man."

"Then tell me. Because it can't be as bad as you think. Not with the way your family looks at you. The way the town sees you."

"I'm not the man you think I am."

"Then tell me who you are. If that's what you think, then tell me."

"I killed a man," he growled out, hating the way her eyes widened for just a bare instant before she schooled her features.

"In the line of duty, I would imagine."

"You say that as if it's duty to take a life." There was nothing in his pledge and oath that could take away the guilt of what he'd done.

"That's not what I meant, and you know it," she said fiercely. "But tell me what happened. Make me understand why you think you're not the man I believe you are or the man I think you could be."

He reached into his back pocket and pulled out his wallet so he could take out the photo he had in there next to the one of his family and Nate. He knew he could keep them on his phone like normal people did now, but he wanted the physical reminder, too.

Before he could show her, however, Kenzie took his hand and moved them both so they could sit on the couch, facing one another. She didn't say a word but took the photo from him when he offered it to her. Once again, she'd done the perfect thing, and once again, he was reminded that he wasn't good enough for her.

"This is…was Jason," he said, pointing at the dark-skinned man in the photo. "You met Jesse already. Jason never got to know Bethany. Both of our women were pregnant at the same time, but only one of us got to see our kid be born."

Kenzie reached out and gripped his hand, settling him so he could continue.

"Jason was a bit older than me, but not by much. Those years though gave him more experience in the field, so I always followed his lead. He was a good man. An honest man. And he died because a drug dealer decided to take the hard way out of a bad situation. He shot Jason in the neck and shot me in the shoulder before I could get a round off and take the guy out. It was the only time I'd ever discharged my weapon out of the range and school. And it was the last time. Backup came soon after, but I was in and out of consciousness since the bullet hit me in just the right place for me to lose a hell of a lot of blood. I could hear Jason beside me, gurgling for breath for a few achingly long moments, but I couldn't move enough to stop the bleeding. Later, they told me I also had a major concussion thanks to hitting the ground as I did when Jason was knocked into me, but I don't know if I can believe that. Not now, looking back. They also told me there was nothing I could have done for the man who was my brother in all but blood."

He didn't cry, didn't put any more emotion into his voice than he normally carried. This was his burden, his mistake, and there was nothing he could do about it. Kenzie watched him, holding his hand while holding the photo with her other hand. She didn't say a word, but he saw the sorrow in her eyes, the pity.

"Jesse came here tonight because she got a letter from the son of the man I killed. The same man who killed her husband, my partner, Jason. I got a letter, too, and will deal with them both tomorrow. But as for Jesse? I don't see her often. I can't. A little over four years ago when Jason died, she didn't want to see me at all. I was too much of a bad memory for her. And I didn't push. I couldn't. Now, she wants to make sure her child knows me because I'm a part of Jason, too, but it's hard, you know? It just reminds me of what we lost and the fact that I'm still here and he isn't."

"Oh, Dare…"

He shook his head. "I lived. Jason didn't. The man I killed didn't either."

"It's not your fault." She squeezed his hand harder, so he didn't interrupt. "What happened was tragic, and my heart hurts for Jesse and her daughter. But my heart also hurts for you and Nate. You've been through so much, Dare, but you've come out the other side. I don't know why you think anything you told me just now would make me not want you…at least not want you for whatever relationship we choose to have." A pause. "Even if that relationship ends up being a friendship and one where we work together and never touch each other again."

He shook his head. "We should want that, we should need

that, yet…"

"And yet… We're making a mistake, aren't we?"

He swallowed hard, remembering once again all the reasons he should say "yes, we are" and walk away. Why he should go back to wondering whom this city girl was and why she was in his space. Instead, he leaned forward, taking the photo from her grasp and carefully placing it on the table in front of him next to his wallet.

"Probably."

"Then why aren't we walking away?"

"Because we're idiots?"

"That…that sounds about right."

"Are we forgetting our problems again? Because I could really use that."

Dare nodded. "That's our plan. Drown in each other, so we don't drown in anything else." With Kenzie, he could *feel* but not feel the dawning darkness that never seemed to go away. He'd take, he'd give, and then he'd walk away when the time came because he didn't know anything else.

He didn't want to think about the letters he'd give his old department. He didn't want to think about the ache in his shoulder or the fact that Jesse had to raise Bethany on her own. He didn't want to think about how Nate was at his *true* home tonight, and that Dare would eventually go home to an empty house. He didn't want to think about the endless paperwork and stress that came from running two business at once when he'd only minored in business rather than his major in criminal justice. He didn't want to think about any of that.

So he leaned down again, this time taking her lips slowly, savoring each and every inch of her. He could drown in her taste, just sink into her and never let go. And while that should scare him, he *couldn't* let her go. Except he wasn't about to do this in her living room on the tiny couch that could barely hold them.

"Your bedroom. Now."

She pulled away, panting, eyes wide. "Okay."

He held back a grin at that because, hell, he knew this was wrong, but he wasn't about to stop it. The two of them were in her bedroom quickly, her shutting the door behind them. If he hadn't already had his mouth on hers and her body pressed close to his, he'd have looked around the place just a bit to check it out, but he couldn't care less right then.

All he wanted was to taste Kenzie, then fill her until they both passed out.

That's what he wanted in the moment, and from the way Red traced her nails down his back through his shirt, she wanted it, too.

Dare led her deeper into the bedroom, keeping his mouth on hers and their hands roaming along each other's bodies. She had a small chaise lounge in the corner of the room, and that gave him ideas. Delicious ones.

"Here?" she asked, letting out a low laugh that went straight to his balls. He stood behind her, pressing her back to his front and rocking his hips slightly.

"Here."

"So, how do you want me?" she asked, turning her head so she could bite his chin. "Like some sweet little regency heroine with my skirt around my hips as I lay thinking of England? Or maybe bent over the back of it?"

He groaned even as he fisted his hand in the fabric of her skirt. "You want to play, then?"

"Let's play."

They stripped each other out of their clothing again, much slower than before, licking and touching as they did. Soon, they were naked, and Dare had her bent over the chaise lounge, on his knees behind her as he licked and sucked at her pussy. He loved eating a woman out, loved having Kenzie's taste on his tongue. She pressed her ass back against him, urging him on as she panted, so he spread her cheeks and fucked her harder with his tongue.

And when she came, yelling his name but not too loudly as the guests could possibly hear her, he stood up, sheathed himself in the condom he'd brought with him, and speared her in the next breath.

She was so damn tight around him. So tight, in fact, that he had to count to ten while he thought of anything but her sweet pussy clamped around his dick.

"I'm going to need to go slow at first, or I won't last long." He groaned when she moved back on his cock, rocking her hips just enough that he practically saw stars. He gripped her hips, but not hard. She said she had issues with anyone gripping her arms, but he wasn't about to test anything else just then. He'd be damned if he hurt her like her fucking ex had.

"Fast. Slow. Don't care. Just *move*."

He grinned at the desperation in her voice since he knew it matched his. And because his lady had asked—no, not *his* lady, *the* lady—he moved. Slow at first, then faster. She moved with him, fucking him just as hard as he fucked her from behind, but no matter how good she felt around him, he wanted to see her face when she came.

"One sec," he growled, pulling all the way out of her.

Then he sat bare-assed naked on the lounge he knew was an antique his family had picked up at some point, and pulled Kenzie onto his lap so she hovered over his dick.

"Ride me, Red."

She licked her lips, gripped the base of his cock, then slowly slid down. "We're defiling this lounge, you know," she said, inching up and then slowly working her way down again.

"I'd say we're not the first, but since I have my dick in you, let's just keep it between us." He said this through gritted teeth since he was now balls-deep in her and ready to come.

"Okay, cowboy, here I go."

"I thought I was a duke in this fantasy," he teased on a moan.

"You're a cowboy visiting regency England, and you found a lovely debutante ready for debauchery." She winked, and he laughed, loving the way she was into this. Into him.

She bounced on his dick, her breasts jiggling and just about sending him over the edge. He had one hand on her hip, keeping her steady so she didn't fall off, and the other on the back of her neck, needing her to keep her gaze on his.

He knew it was a mistake, knew it would be too intimate when they came together, but he didn't care in the heat of the moment.

So when they came, calling each other's names in frantic whispers, he knew he had to walk away before things got even more complicated.

But he wouldn't.

Not yet.

Because, like he'd told himself before, he was a selfish bastard.

10

"GET YOUR ASS up off the couch and get yourself a beer," Dare growled at Fox. His mood had been shit when he walked into Fox's place an hour before and, apparently, it had only gotten worse since.

Fox nudged him in the shoulder and glared down at him. "Really? Keep your yelling at the TV and Mario Kart and not me, especially *not* in my house. I don't know what's crawled up your ass, but you can just fuck right off."

"Could be the fact that we're in our thirties and playing Mario Kart," Dare grumbled, annoyed with himself. He *liked* playing Mario Kart, but now he was just picking a fight because he couldn't find a way to fight about anything else. Between the three of them, they had a hundred games to play of various types and strengths but to start with for their rare joint afternoon off, they'd gone with something fun that would easily lead to more cursing and throwing things than any other hardcore game they had.

"Could be you're freaking out since you're sleeping with the innkeeper," Loch drawled from his seat in the leather recliner. He had his attention on the screen in front of him as he chose a rider and vehicle. Loch was a very serious player, even when it came to a game from their childhood.

Fox sat up and grabbed the controller from Dare's hand. Dare looked over at his younger brother and glared. "You're sleeping with Kenzie? When did this happen?"

"I thought you were the reporter," Loch said, taking the remote from Fox so he could lower the volume. "Shouldn't you know these things before me?"

"I haven't been by the bar in over a week since we're on deadline with this special edition and all the other shit I have to do when I have two copy editors and my sports reporter down with a virus." Fox glared over at Loch before turning back to Dare. "And you and Kenzie? I knew you two were sniffing around each other, but I didn't know it had gotten that serious."

"It's not serious." His brothers just stared at him when he said it. "It can't be." That was the truth, even though he had a feeling neither of his brothers actually believed him. Hell, he wasn't sure he and Kenzie believed each other, but he'd be damned if he let it be anything else.

Fox held up one finger. "First, sex when it comes to you, is always serious. Even if you tell yourself that you're a free man since Monica, it's serious. Hell, you were practically married to her without the vows, no matter what she said."

"Is there a second to this diatribe of yours?" Dare asked. "And you're wrong about whatever the hell you just said." He was glad he didn't have a controller in his hand right then, or he'd probably brain Fox with it or crack it in his grip.

"I'm never wrong. Second," Fox said, using his middle finger to point rather than holding up two fingers. Classy. "You wouldn't be all grumbly and growly and getting on my last ever-loving nerve if getting it on with the innkeeper didn't mean something."

"Her name is Kenzie. Stop calling her *the innkeeper* like that's all she is or some shit."

Fox and Dare gave each other knowing looks.

Idiots.

"What?"

"You're mighty defensive over a woman you say you're not getting serious with." Fox leaned back into the corner of the couch and raised a brow in Dare's direction.

"Shut it. I don't want to talk about it, okay?"

"We're here if you want to, you know," Loch put in, his voice low. "You might be growling right now, but you're still smiling more than ever before at the bar when I'm there working on the inn."

"Maybe it's you," Dare deadpanned. "I'm just glad to see my family."

Loch flipped him off before turning back to the TV. "If that's what you tell yourself so you can sleep at night."

Dare couldn't sleep at night, not with dreams of Kenzie mixing with the night he'd gotten shot. That was the problem.

"Dare?" Fox asked, all teasing out of his tone.

"What?" he growled.

"Kenzie is all high-class and a pretty amazing woman."

"And? You think I'm not good enough for her? I know that, dipshit."

Loch just sighed, and Fox glared. "No, that's not what I'm saying, you ass. What I'm saying is that you two are pretty good for each other. At least on the outside looking in." He paused. "I just don't want you hurt again. Okay?"

Dare didn't say anything, not sure what there was to say after that, so he took the controller back from Fox and went to select his player. "Anything but Rainbow Road, okay? I hate that one."

"There're like four Rainbow Roads on this version," Loch pointed out. "They took some of the old console layouts and added them into this one, just a little smoother."

"So none of the Rainbow Roads." If he focused on petty crap like that, he could at least breathe for the afternoon. He had no idea what the hell he was going to do about Kenzie or his life for that matter. He might as well play games with his brothers for the two hours he had off and just forget what else was going on in the world around him.

Because his brothers knew him, they stopped asking him about Kenzie for the time being. Instead, they tried to beat the hell out of each other with each game they played within the small break they had. Dare knew Loch had to go and pick up Misty from her friend's house soon—a friend who had a very single mother that seemed to want to get in Loch's pants, but his brother wasn't interested as far as Dare could tell. Fox had work to do as usual, and Dare was surprised his brother had even taken time to sit around and do nothing for as long as he had. Fox was constantly moving and reading, doing his job and loving it.

Dare, on the other hand, might work his ass off, but sometimes he didn't particularly like it. It was hard work, and he was good at it, but it wasn't the only thing he loved in the world. Anyone who adored every aspect of his or her job was one lucky asshole.

Their father showed up about an hour into their game time and joined in with gusto. *This* was why Dare knew he'd been an asshole when his parents told them they were hiring Kenzie. His parents needed the time off to relax and just *be*. And what had he done? Gotten all butt hurt over the fact that his parents hadn't told him about their plans for *their* business. It was any wonder his mother hadn't lashed his hide right then.

"How's Nate doing?" Bob asked soon after he'd arrived. "You're getting him soon, right?"

Dare nodded, taking a sip of his soda. "Next weekend. He's good. We talked last night for almost an hour. If he wasn't so young, I'd totally get him a cell phone so we could text, but that might be pushing it."

"Considering I didn't let *you* get one until college, I feel like an old man."

"There were only a few kids who had those old Nokia phones in high school. They didn't become a big thing until like freshman year of college for me, and then came the flip phones." He snorted. "The insanity of the flip phone was over quickly compared to when the touchscreen came out."

"You kids and your technology."

"Says the man who killed it at Candy Crush before the rest of us had even downloaded the app."

His dad just grinned. "I'm good. What can I say? Plus, it was candy without the calories that could lead to the infamous Collins gut." He pointed at Dare's stomach. "Better watch out with all that whiskey of yours."

Dare patted his flat belly. "Keep dreaming. I do pretty well for myself."

Loch snorted. "If you or Fox ever came to my gym and punched a few bags, you might actually have some muscle."

"I like my leanness, thank you very much," Fox said, his attention on the TV in front of him.

"You say leanness, I say skinny ass arms." Loch's lips

twitched, and Dare full-out grinned. They just needed Tabby and his mom here, and it would be a perfect family afternoon. Of course, if Tabby were here, she'd beat them all as Link or Princess Peach since that girl had the best Mario Kart moves of the four of them.

Twenty minutes later, he left the guys playing another game since he had to go to work. Rick was on shift at the bar that night, but Dare still needed to be there to oversee things. Plus, Claire had mentioned there might be an issue with his chef's attitude, and that wasn't something he was in the mood to deal with in the middle of a rush, so he'd get there and see what he could do before they were fully open. He knew Loch would only stay at Fox's for probably another ten minutes and then he'd head over to pick up Misty and then go into work. Fox, on the other hand, would probably find a way to keep working while they let their dad play. Dad didn't get enough time with each of them, so they'd make it work.

Rick was behind the bar finishing up the last of the lunch stragglers when Dare walked in. Claire, on the other hand, was right at the kitchen entrance, fists on her hips.

"I don't care if you want to try a new recipe. You want to do that? You tell me *before* shift starts and when I can order at cost. You don't tell me *after* everything is printed and ingredients are not only hard to come by but also pricey as hell."

She had her voice low so it wouldn't carry to any of the people in the bar or the inn above, but Dare was still pissed that she had to deal with any of it at all.

"What's going on?" Dare asked, frowning as he watched Griz, their top chef and genuine pain the ass, growl behind the stove.

"I'm a chef. An *artist*. I don't need to be held back by socie-ty's norms."

Dare pinched the bridge of his nose and prayed for patience. "Did you really just say artist? And society's norms? We're a restaurant. We make steak, chicken, fish, pork, a vegetarian option, and an exotic option like pheasant or wild boar if we feel like it. That's it. You dress it up. You make it taste phenomenal because that's what you do damn well, but you don't fuck with shit."

"Art. Ist." Griz said the word in two syllables that made him sound like an ass, not an award-winning chef. Though, really, those two weren't exclusive.

"He ordered the rainbow trout and didn't tell me," Claire growled. "He had it *overnighted* for tomorrow so he could make a special he's been dreaming of. He did it on his own, Dare. And I'm going to kill him."

"No bloodshed," Dare warned. "We don't want the mess or the paperwork."

"Griz? For fuck's sake. Really? If you wanted the trout, just tell us, we'd do it for next week. We don't overnight ingredients we aren't prepared for because you're in a mood. And we damn well don't waste money. Got me?"

"I can't send it back," Griz growled. "Nor can I cancel the order. It's too late."

Claire started grumbling under her breath, and Dare shook his head. He'd been a cop, that was what he'd thought he was good at. This? Fuck, he hated when he felt out of his depth even though he'd trained to run the businesses, as well.

"This is the *last* time you do this. You do it again, and you're looking for a new job." He held up his hand when both of them started complaining. "I won't take the extra costs out of your pay, but you *will* do whatever Claire needs you to for the next week in addition to your extra duties. I've been lax on your time because you and Claire do good work, but I'm not in the mood for petty bullshit. You got me?" Griz nodded, his face set in straight lines. "And if you talk to Claire again like you were when I walked in here, you're gone."

With that, he stormed back into his office, Claire on his tail. "I can handle him usually, but sometimes I know he gets pissy that he has to answer to a woman."

Dare shook his head and searched through a few files for the one he was looking for. He had a shit-ton of paperwork to get done before he worked the floor, and he already had a headache from hell.

"You can handle him always, but right then, it wasn't about him not listening to you because you were a woman. He did something against the business as a whole, that's why I spoke up. I'd usually leave it to you to deal with because you can handle it, but I couldn't just then."

"And I get that," Claire said. "If I felt like you were trying to protect me because I'm the little woman, I'd have said something."

He snorted, a smile twitching at his lips. "I don't doubt it. You'd probably have kicked my ass on the way."

"True enough." She let out a breath, her shoulders relaxing slightly before she pulled herself back up. "Okay, then. Time to get to work and make the place shine. By the way, your innkeeper was down here earlier, walking guests through the place and setting up reservations. She's damn good at her job." She gave him a knowing smile, and he narrowed his eyes.

"She's not my innkeeper."

She just smiled at him. "I meant your family's innkeeper, but...interesting. Very interesting." She drew out the word, and he went back to his paperwork.

"Don't you have a restaurant to manage or something?"

"I might. I just might." She laughed on her way out of his office, and he glowered. Was he that transparent? He and Kenzie were just...well, he didn't know what to call them, but they weren't serious.

They weren't.

And the mix of laughter and doubt in his head could just back the fuck off.

Knowing he only had about forty-five minutes to get some work done before he was needed out front, he sat down and pulled out some of his paperwork. And because he was a glutton for punishment, he also pulled out his phone and sent a quick text.

Dare: *In the office. Hope you're having a better day.*

Kenzie: *Doing okay. We're full-up tonight so that makes me happy. I'm about to show one of the new couples around the area a bit since I need a walk. Then I have paperwork so I'll eat upstairs while I do it. Fun, right?*

Dare: *Sounds like my life.*

Kenzie: *Yay us for being adults.*

He shook his head and pushed his phone away so he wouldn't be tempted to text her again. He didn't know why had in the first place, other than the fact that he hadn't wanted her to hear he was in the building from anyone else.

He just kept making one mistake after another it seemed,

and it didn't look as if he were going to quit anytime soon.

"Idiot," he mumbled and got to work.

Right when he was about to head back out into the front to see how things were going, his phone rang. This time, he smiled wide and picked up, eager to hear the voice on the other end.

"Daddy? Mommy let me call all on my own!

"Nate, my man. How's it hangin'?"

"Today I picked up a rolly bug that made Mommy squeal. And then I helped Daddy Auggie with his books. Oh and then I talked to Misty on the phone because she was with her friend that she says isn't as good a friend as I am but she still thinks that her friend is great. That means I'm great too, right? And then I played in the outside again because I was being too loud with the blocks and trains but I like outside because the leaves are different colors and soon I get to play in them. Oh, and Mommy says I get to get a new bed soon because I'm too big for my other bed. I'm a big boy now. Mommy and Grandma say so."

All of this was said in one or two breaths, and Dare was frankly concerned his son might not be getting enough oxygen to his brain. He also didn't correct any of his grammar since Monica was right by him, and he could hear her subtle corrections on the other end of the phone.

"You sound like you had a productive day." Tiring, yet Dare could only think of how nice it would have been to play video games with his son *and* brothers instead of having to hear about Nate's activities in passing. *One day*, he reminded himself. One day, things might change.

He hoped, at least.

Of course, the idea of the letters he'd dropped off at the precinct reminded him that he still wasn't exactly safe for his kid, at least according to Monica. He hadn't told her about it since he was sure nothing would come of it, and the detectives on the case were now keeping an eye out, but still, Dare had the thoughts of what could happen to his family if his past life came back circling in his mind.

Maybe there was a reason he hadn't gotten full custody.

And that was exactly why he should stay away from Kenzie.

Full. Fucking. Circle.

He talked to Nate a little longer, soaking up each word and moment he had with his son, then sat there a few minutes after they'd hung up so he could gather his thoughts. He had work to do, and a life to live, but damned if he didn't want to throw it all away and find time to be with Nate.

Custody agreements, and life in general, sucked sometimes, and Dare knew he needed to stop whining about what he didn't have and learn to live with what he did.

"Enough," he growled and headed out to the front so he could do what he did best—clean up messes.

By the time he was done for the day, his limbs were heavy, and he just wanted a cold beer and his bed. But since he had to wake up early for inventory in the morning, he said no to the beer and headed straight to bed.

As soon as he lay naked between his sheets, he thought of Kenzie and grabbed his phone from the nightstand. He hadn't closed, so it wasn't that late. Hopefully, if she were asleep, she wouldn't hear the vibrations from her text, but he didn't think she'd be in bed yet.

Dare: *You awake?*

His phone rang instead of a text back, and he answered right away. "Hey."

"Hey, there. I'm just about to go to bed, and I wasn't in the mood to text." Her voice held that smooth-as-whiskey tone, and it went straight to his balls.

"I hate talking on the phone, but I think I hate texting more."

"That sounds about right," she said on a laugh. "How was your day?"

He told her about his time with his family, then his call with Nate, and work. When he mentioned Griz, she sighed, and he could see her shaking her head in his mind.

"That man makes *amazing* food, but I don't know how you deal with him."

"One day at a time, I guess. He's not always that much of an ass."

"That's good to know."

She told him about her day and some of the guests that had shown up throughout the afternoon. When she talked about upcoming renovations, he nodded along, putting in a few of his own observations since he knew the building so well. And all the while, he kept asking himself why they were talking like this.

If they weren't serious, why were they talking about their days? Why did he need to hear her voice before he slept?

They should keep it casual...or stop altogether, yet Dare wasn't sure he could do the latter.

Which was why he said, "Go out with me tomorrow."

She paused. "What?"

"Go out on a date with me tomorrow."

"We're dating?"

"I have no idea, but I want to take you to dinner. What do you say?"

She was silent for so long, he was sure he'd fucked up. "Okay."

He blinked. "Okay?"

"Yeah, okay."

"Okay."

He blew out a breath, oddly relieved. They talked for a few minutes more before hanging up, his eyes heavy. He knew they were both sending mixed signals, but at this point, he wasn't sure he could stop.

There was just something about his innkeeper that made him keep going, mistake or not.

11

KENZIE HADN'T STOPPED moving since she woke up that morning. It seemed like every guest needed to check out at the exact same time, and the next sets arrived soon after—all needing exact and very particular things.

Her feet ached, and her back throbbed, but damned if she was going to fail any of her guests. This was her job, and something she excelled at, if she did say so herself, even if she truly wanted some wine. Only forty more minutes, and then she could have all she wanted. Or at least a glass since she still had things to do to prep for her date with Dare.

A date.

How on earth had she ended up saying yes to a date with him? And why had he even asked in the first place?

Deep breaths, Kenzie. This was fine. Everything was fine.

It was just dinner. They'd had sex for freak's sake. He'd tasted every inch of her body, so if he wanted to buy her dinner, why not? They'd already eaten meals together at the bar while he was working and with friends. This should be no different.

Except it was, and they both knew it. But seeing how neither of them was backing away, maybe they could do this. What *this* was, she didn't know, but it wasn't as if she *ever* truly had a clue what she was doing beyond work. Outside of organizing the inn, she felt like she was out of her depth.

She'd come to Whiskey to find a new life and community. She hadn't come to find a best friend she immediately clicked with like Ainsley, or a family that seemed to want to take her under their wing as the Collinses did. She liked every single member of the family with fervor, even Tabby, who she hadn't yet met but whom she had talked to on the phone more than once. And they'd clicked since the woman was apparently a planner and organization like Kenzie. Barbara had made sure the two could connect, and Kenzie was happy for it.

She definitely hadn't come to Whiskey to find a man who she could fall for, and she was so scared that she had.

She'd already lost herself once before to a man, and she still hadn't quite untangled herself from the ramifications of that relationship. And while Dare was nothing, *nothing* like David, she still wasn't sure she could ever fully open up her heart again. Dare didn't need a woman who couldn't be completely his. He already had that with his ex and, frankly, his job. He didn't need Kenzie while she was still figuring out who she was without the chains and shackles of a loveless, abusive marriage.

"Miss?"

She looked up at a middle-aged couple who had checked in an hour before and smiled. "Yes, Mr. and Mrs. Snow, how can I help you?"

Mr. Snow smiled. "We have reservations tomorrow night in the Whiskey Restaurant downstairs, but we don't have plans tonight since we weren't sure what time we'd be getting in due to traffic and all that."

"Roger here tends to have a lead foot," Mrs. Snow said with a laugh.

Roger just rolled his eyes, and Kenzie couldn't help but smile at the love and affection the two of them had for one another. When she was younger, she'd told herself that was what she wanted. As she'd grown older and into her marriage with David, she realized that she'd never have that. Now, she wasn't sure about anything anymore.

"I have a few places that might fit what you need, and since it's only Thursday night, you most likely won't need reservations." She reached under her antique desk in the entryway and pulled out a few menus. "It's also a bit early, of course, so whatever you choose, I can call ahead for you and put your name in."

"Oh, really?" the other woman asked before browsing through the papers in front of her.

"It's what I'm here for." She went through each of the menus with the couple as neither of them knew what they were in the mood for. When they finally made their decision, the couple left to walk down Main Street while Kenzie called the restaurant and put in the couple's name for later.

Of course, going through all the options for food in Whiskey only made her stomach rumble, and she was glad when she could end her shift for the day and head upstairs to get ready for her date with Dare. He was taking her to Marsha Brown's, a Cajun place right off Main street known for its delicious food. She'd yet to go there for even lunch, but every time she walked by, she could scent the spices and her mouth watered. She honestly couldn't wait to try out their menu.

Of course, she hoped her stomach would be able to handle the heavy food since it was still in knots over the idea of a date with Dare to begin with.

"Let's do this," she muttered to herself as she stood in front of her closet, figuring out what she was going to wear. Before she could choose, however, there was a knock on the door. She hoped it wasn't Dare showing up forty-five minutes early. Not likely, but with that man, she never did know.

Ainsley stood in the hall when she opened the door, a grin on her face and two bottles of adult root beer in her hand. "I heard you were prepping for your date with *Dare*," she said the word slowly and fluttered her eyelashes, making Kenzie laugh, "so I thought I'd show up to do the friend thing and help you pick out what to wear." She wiggled her hand. "And I brought hard root beer because it won't make you buzzed, and it's yummy."

Kenzie took a step back and let the other woman in, a grin on her face. "I *love* hard root beer and most other hard sodas. If it weren't for the fact that I'm drinking two months' worth of sugar in one bottle, I'd have them daily."

Ainsley just winked and set the bottles on Kenzie's counter. "It's a special occasion. An actual *date* with Dare Collins." She fanned herself. "Ooh la la."

Kenzie just shook her head, a smile playing on her lips even as, inside, she was far too stressed to even *think* about joking.

"It's just a date. Dinner. We've eaten together before." Kenzie held up a red tunic and leggings combo, and Ainsley shook her head.

"You've done dinner where you sit at a bar and he works, or you eat with me or one of his brothers there. You've even eaten with *Nate,* but you've never been on a real date with Nate's dad."

Kenzie swallowed hard. That was true, and she'd even just told herself something along those lines. She was about to go on a real date with a single father who happened to make her knees shake. Once again, she had to ask herself how on earth this had happened.

Not knowing what else to say, she reached into her closet and pulled out the green dress she'd worn when she first met him. It was her favorite, and she *knew* the man liked her in it since she'd been aware of how he watched her legs. She might as well feel comfortable when she was on edge.

Ainsley grinned and held two thumbs up. "Perfect. Now, root beer and makeup and then I'll leave."

"I don't know what I'd do without you."

The other woman just shrugged. "You're in Whiskey now. You'll never have to know."

And that thought warmed Kenzie far more than she thought it could. She was in Whiskey, her new home. She had a new job, a new set of friends, and was going on a date with a new man. She wasn't the same woman anymore. And maybe, just maybe, tonight was exactly what she needed.

Dare knocked on the door right on time, and she blew out a breath while running her hands over a non-existent wrinkle before opening the door. He stood there, his eyes going dark as he ran his gaze over her, and she licked her lips. He looked damn good in stone grey pants and a black, button-down shirt. The clothes were just fitted enough that she could see his muscles and that made her mouth water.

How on earth was this her life?

"You look...wow." He looked her up and down, a delicious grin on his face. "That dress. Did you know I've had fantasies of you in this?"

She snorted. "Uh, not so much about the fantasies part, but I saw the way you looked at me in the bar that first night."

"And you still gave me that dismissive look."

She winced as she closed the door behind her. "I didn't mean to look so bitchy. I had other things on my mind."

He took her hand, and she swallowed hard. They were holding hands and walking down to their date. Once again, she had to question how this was her life now.

"Don't call yourself bitchy. You were nothing of the sort. You were damn sexy. *Are* damn sexy."

"You're not too bad yourself," she said on a laugh and leaned into his shoulder. She could do this, she thought. She could go out on a date with an attractive man and just enjoy herself for the evening. She didn't have to think about what-ifs and what path she was taking. She could just *be* for the evening and let everything else fall where it may around her.

Tomorrow, she could stress out about everything else. Tonight, she would just be Kenzie. The Kenize on a date with Dare.

As they stood at a crosswalk, waiting for the light to change and traffic to pass, Dare leaned into her and kissed the top of her head. It was such a casual gesture that she wasn't sure he even realized he'd done it. And because she wasn't sure what to do with whatever it meant, she told herself she'd live in the now like she'd promised herself for so long. That no matter what happened tonight, and after tonight, she wouldn't let herself fall into the abyss of worry. She'd spent so many years worrying, it was time to just be. At least for an evening.

Marsha Brown's was on the opposite side of the street as the inn, so it faced the river but wasn't backed up against it for the view. Instead, huge trees surrounded the back so it looked mysterious and yet welcoming with its open doors and smiling hostesses. Kenzie was pretty sure the building had once been a church with its high ceilings and tower, but over time, it had transformed into a gorgeous restaurant with ornate carvings and a huge painting the size of two walls in the back. It was an experience for sure.

"So I need the shrimp?" she asked after the waiter brought their wine. "That's what you said, right?"

"Anything here is pretty fantastic. If we come during lunch, the Po' Boys are as big as my head." He used his hands to gesture, and she laughed. "Seriously, though. They have some spicy things, and I know that's not your favorite, but others are pretty delicious and savory rather than spicy."

She frowned. "How did you know I don't like spicy?"

He shrugged, his attention on his menu before he looked up and met her eyes. "Ainsley puts hot sauce on top of her oysters and makes sure not to let it splash anywhere near your half when you guys share an appetizer. I thought maybe you were allergic to vinegar or something, but you had it on your salad once, so I figured it was because of the heat level."

He'd been far more observant than she'd thought, and she couldn't help but warm at the idea that he watched her—not in a creepy way, of course, but in a way that meant he knew little things about her beyond how she felt in bed.

"I can't do too spicy," Kenzie finally said, pushing thoughts of what it could mean out of her head. He was a bartender and a former cop, after all. Being observant was in his nature.

"Then try the gumbo to start," Dare said, gesturing with his menu. "They make it with chicken here, and I just about slide out of my seat from the flavors. They have two pots of it at all times, one spicy, one not, so you won't have to worry."

Her stomach rumbled at the thought of gumbo, and she licked her lips. "And now I'm starving."

"Then I guess we came to the right place."

She smiled, setting down her menu. "I guess we did."

By the time they were stuffed on chicken gumbo, and pecan pie, Kenzie was warm and full and snuggling into Dare's side as they made their way back to the inn. For as much as she told herself what she had with Dare couldn't be serious, she was acting pretty serious right now, but she would ignore it and just think of the good food in her belly and what the two of them were about to do once they got up to her room.

"Did I tell you that you look damn sexy in that dress?" Dare asked. "Because, hell, Kenzie. The first time I saw you in it, I couldn't breathe. Now? Now I just want to slide it up your hips and fuck you deep and hard while you're wearing it."

They were once again standing at the crosswalk, and he was whispering into her ear. It took all that was within her not to jump him right there. Instead, she stood just a bit straighter so she couldn't tempt herself, and gently pressed her thighs together to try and ease the ache. Dare's eyes narrowed at the action, and a pleased smirk slid over his face.

"Don't," she whispered fiercely. "Smug isn't a good look on you."

He leaned in again so no one would hear. "Then you'd better wipe it off my face. Preferably by sitting on it."

She blinked up at him, his words taking a second to catch up with her brain, and as soon as they did, she threw her head back and laughed.

He mock-scowled at her before pulling her across the street

when the light turned green. "I wasn't kidding, Ms. Owens."

"Oh, I know you weren't," she said, wiping a tear from her eye. "And I plan on doing just that in like ten minutes, but you're still adorable."

He snorted. "I'm not adorable. I'm ruggedly handsome and growly. Nate is adorable."

She smiled at the thought of his son. "Yeah, Nate *is* adorable. Did he finish his project?" Dare's son had been asked to draw his home and family for his pre-K class. She knew Dare had been worried about it, not because of Nate's aptitude, but because Dare wasn't sure where he fit in Nate's idea of family. She didn't know why she'd even asked tonight since they had been having such a nice time, and now she was afraid she'd ruined it, but there was no going back.

Dare smiled softly at her. "He got a perfect gold star like I knew he would. He ended up drawing *two* houses on one page and put himself in both next to each of us. Yeah, he drew Auggie, but the guy isn't a bad stepfather, so I guess that's okay."

Kenzie was pretty sure her heart grew three sizes just like the Grinch at Dare's answer. "He drew both?"

Dare squeezed her to his side as they walked into the bar and inn. "Yeah, he drew both. Nate's pretty damn amazing."

"Well, he takes after his father." She winked as Dare just rolled his eyes. "I'm telling you the truth, you know. You might only get him one weekend a month, but you're still in his life. He knows who you are and how much you're trying. That counts for something."

Dare nodded but didn't say anything, and she knew she'd have to get off this track of conversation. After all, they weren't serious, no matter how confusing her feelings may be at the moment.

She was saved from having to come up with a new direction in conversation as Claire came up to Dare, a pleasant smile on her face but panic in her eyes. Considering Kenzie was pretty sure she'd never seen Claire panic, *ever*, she knew something had to be going on that would need Dare's attention.

"Can I talk to you a minute?" Claire asked Dare. "Sorry, Kenzie. I'd handle it on my own if I could." And considering that up to this moment, Kenzie had thought Claire could deal with *anything*, that was saying something.

"No problem," Kenzie said quickly. "I'll go up and see how everyone is doing." She looked at Dare. "Meet me at my place when you can?"

Dare gave her a quick nod before going to help Claire with whatever she needed. Knowing it might be a while and their date might have to end a bit early, she waved at Rick on her way past the bar and made her way up the wide staircase in the back where her new home and inn were. She loved the set up of Old Whiskey, even though it had been a little weird to get used to at first. She was slowly becoming part of the town, and she knew she'd made the right decision in leaving the city—and David— and coming to Pennsylvania.

For the first time in a long while, while she might not have her life perfectly planned out in front of her, she was happy.

Happy.

When she reached the top of the staircase, there was a man standing by the front desk, but no one was there to help him. Annoyed at her night staff and herself for letting this happen, she walked right up to the man, a smile on her face.

"Hello, how can I help you?"

The man turned, and blood rushed from her face.

He lifted a lip in a snarl as his gaze traveled over her body. She needed to shower. Needed to wash herself of him. But she couldn't move. She couldn't do anything. She could only stand there as he studied her and apparently found her lacking.

"David."

12

"KENZIE." DAVID'S VOICE was low, and it shook her bones, filling her belly with dread.

"What are you doing here?" she asked, proud of herself for being able to push through the terror and speak at all. She wasn't that woman anymore, she reminded herself. She wouldn't bow down to this man simply because he looked at her so intently. He could yell and scream all he wanted if he got up to that point, and she wouldn't back down.

She wasn't that Kenzie anymore.

She just had to remember that now that he stood in front of her. There was no ignoring his calls or his presence when he was so close. There was no disregarding *him*.

"My wife is here. Where else would I be?"

Kenzie tilted her head, doing her best to look nonchalant and not like she wanted to run away. "Oh? Did you get married again?"

"Don't sound so flippant. It's not becoming."

"I'm not your wife any longer. You and I both signed the papers. I'm going to ask you again. Why are you here?"

"You said your vows to me. You promised to obey. We're still married in the eyes of God."

She shook her head, wanting a way out of this conversation

in any way possible. "You haven't been in a church since our wedding day. Don't throw vows and religion at me to suit your own needs. *It's not becoming*," she said, echoing his words.

David snarled and took a step toward her. She moved back without thinking, hating herself for doing it and for the way pleasure gleamed in his eyes.

"You need to leave, David. I live and work here. You aren't my husband anymore, and you have no right to be in my space. Just go."

"And what if I wanted a room in this fleabag you call an inn? Shouldn't you be accommodating?"

"We have no vacancies," she lied. They had one room left, but she'd be damned if she let him anywhere near it.

"Don't fucking lie to me," he growled, moving toward her in a swift movement. He had his hands around her arms in an instant, and she froze, ice in her veins, her throat closing up at the contact.

She'd dreamed of this, had nightmares about this terror, this pain, this touch.

Yet she couldn't wake up because this wasn't a dream. Somehow, he had her against the wall, slamming her head back so hard she clacked her back teeth together.

"You'll come back, Kenzie. You'll do as you're told, and you'll come back. I let you play because I'm forgiving, but I'm done being that man. I'm done letting you whore yourself out to anyone who dares touch what's *mine*. You're coming with me, and that's the end of it." He slammed her back into the wall again, his hands squeezing her upper arms so tightly she knew he'd leave bruises.

"Let me go," she said, finding the courage that had helped

her leave him in the first place. "You're making a mistake by touching me."

He let go of one arm only to slap her face. She blinked rapidly, the sting spreading through her skin as she fought to remain calm. If she let him see her panic, he'd hurt her more. That was how he'd done it in the past with his words, and she *knew* his hands would be the same.

"Bitch."

Rage filled her at that word, knowing Dare had just told her not to call herself one. Besides, she'd hated it to begin with.

She tried to wiggle out of David's hold, her arms aching, and her face pulsating where he'd hit her. He wouldn't let her go, but because she'd jostled their positions just enough, she was able to raise her knee and slam it into his balls. He fell back, cursing while holding his crotch, and she went to run around him. She'd go downstairs and get help. With the noise of the bar and restaurant, no one had been able to hear anything that had happened so far, so she'd have to fight for herself—something she'd been trying to do all along.

But before she could make it to the stairs, David had his hand on her hair and pulled her back. Her heel caught on the top stair, and she fell, her hands reaching out to break her fall as her ankle twisted. The movement made his hold on her hair tighten, and he pulled harder, dragging her a foot across the carpeted floor as she tried to get away.

She screamed then, knowing that if she didn't, there was no way anyone could hear her. She just prayed someone would hear her over the din of noise below.

"Help! Let go of me!"

David pulled harder.

She tried to tug herself away, rolling on her hands and knees, twisting her hair in the process, but he held on. Before she could panic more than she already was and start screaming again, Dare was at her side.

The hold on her hair loosened, and she fell back hard. Dare had David down on the ground and had already punched him twice in the face by the time Kenzie was able to look up and stagger over.

"Stop, Dare. Don't kill him. He's not worth it."

She had her hand on Dare's shoulder, her body aching as she shook, and Dare stopped in an instant.

"Call the cops," he growled out. "This bastard is getting locked up."

"Already on it," Rick said quickly from behind them. "Get your lady, Dare. I'll hold this piece of shit down until the cops come and take him."

"I'll sue you," David growled through his bloody lips. "I'll sue all of you. That's my fucking *wife*."

Dare stood up, his hands fisted at his sides. The look he gave her was fierce and full of emotion, she blinked, tears stinging her eyes. But she would not cry in front of these people. She might be able to break down in front of Dare behind closed doors, but even then, she wasn't sure. She wasn't sure of anything anymore.

She'd thought she had left her past behind her, yet it seemed no matter how far she'd come, how far she'd run, David would always be there, lurking and ready to strike.

"You're shaking," Dare growled out as he stalked toward her. She didn't jump at his tone, and she was glad for it. It wasn't his fault that she was jumpy, but she knew if she looked like she was ready to break, he'd find a way to blame himself. It was what he did.

She wouldn't be his burden to bear, no matter how easy it was to learn to lean on him.

"I'm fine," she said, not quite knowing if it was a lie or not.

He lowered his brows and gently brought her into his arms. She rested the good side of her face on his chest, his heartbeat a rapid yet steady pulse beneath her cheek. "You're not fine," he said, low, his voice devoid of emotion.

"I can't...I can't talk right now." Others had joined them in the hallway. People she worked with on a daily basis, as well as guests and people who had come into the building for dinner. She wanted to hide from all of them and not let them see what she'd brought with her. She'd done so well keeping that part of her past out of her present, yet there was no denying what had happened tonight.

She might have been able to fight back this evening, but she hadn't been strong enough to do anything except scream. Loch came up the stairs, fury in his gaze as he met Kenzie's eyes, but he didn't say anything.

No one said anything.

What was there to say?

Soon, the cops were there, and they seemed to know Dare. They ushered almost everyone out of the area and carted David off. Then they took her statement while Dare held her before they went to the others to get theirs. She barely heard what they told her, but she had a feeling that even if they promised they'd take care of her ex-husband, this wouldn't be the last she heard from him.

Even assault wouldn't keep him away from her and in jail for long, not with his money and connections. That was why she'd run, after all, wasn't it? Because she hadn't been able to stay in her old home and city even with his documented abuse. When it came to those in power—and money was power no matter what others said—the system didn't work the same. It failed her every time she tried to fight back.

And she knew Dare understood. He'd been part of that same system and had still lost those he cared about and had bled for the cause, only to walk away when he thought he wasn't enough.

Over two hours later, she was at Dare's house and in his living room, while Loch leaned against the wall, his arms folded over his large chest. While she could have stayed at her apartment, she was glad Dare had insisted that they come to his place rather than staying at the inn. She'd go back tomorrow. She had a job to do and a life to live.

And no matter what, she had to remember that she'd fought back.

It might not have been enough, *but she'd fought back.*

"Mom and Dad are going to call you tomorrow," Dare said as he paced in front of her. She'd have preferred him sitting beside her, but she knew he had too much restless energy at the moment to do that. "They called earlier once they heard, but I convinced them, Fox, Tabby, and Ainsley to give you some space tonight." He gave Loch a pointed look, and his brother just shrugged.

Kenzie felt a little slow as she took it all in but nodded. "I hate that I worried them."

Dare gave her a sharp look. "You didn't do a damn thing. It's not your fault."

She just nodded. "I know that. But I still brought it with me."

"Your ex did that," Loch put in before pushing off from the wall. "You fought back and did well. If you want to learn more, not just because of tonight, but in general, come to the gym and take one of the classes. You're one of us, Kenzie. We're not going to let this happen to you again."

With that, he gave her a nod and distance, leaving the house quietly without saying anything to Dare. Somehow, his gruff demeanor and the way he wanted her to learn to fight back helped her settle down so she could talk to Dare. This family confused her most days, yet they comforted her at the same time. They were always there for each other, and the fact that Loch had called her one of them meant something.

But now that he was gone, she had to deal with Dare. Because no matter what Loch said, it was the two of them that decided what she was to him and his family, what she was to *Dare*.

And all of that combined with what had happened tonight gave her a headache. Of course, that could have been because she'd hit her head, as well. Or rather David had *slammed* her head against the wall.

Jesus, what a night.

"Do you want some water?" Dare asked, his voice toneless.

She looked up at him. "I'm fine. Sit down, Dare. You don't need to keep pacing."

"If I don't pace, I'll yell, and you don't need me yelling at you."

She raised her brow. "Why would you feel the need to yell at me?"

He sighed, running a hand through his short hair. "Not *at* you. Hell, you didn't do anything wrong. I just meant yelling when you're around. I'm so fucking pissed off, Kenzie. That man was in my building, *our* building, and I didn't know. He hurt you, and I didn't know. He was going to do worse and if I hadn't been at the bottom of the stairs when you yelled for me. I might not have known. And then what did I do? I came in and hit him. I fucking hit him in front of you, and you can't even look at me because I hit someone just like he did. I'm so damn sorry, Kenzie."

She stood up at his words, moving around the coffee table so she could put her hands on his chest. "That was a lot...I mean...Dare? None of that was on you. None of it is on me either."

"And you shouldn't have to be the one comforting me." He leaned his head down on hers and cupped her un-bruised cheek. "Damn it, Kenzie. I could have lost you tonight."

Her body shuddered. "But you didn't. I'm still here. And I hurt him, Dare. I didn't just stand there. And I'm grateful you were there, too. What you did to protect me is nothing like what David did to hurt me. I hope you realize that."

He blew out a breath, the warmth sliding over her skin. "You fought back. I'm so damn proud of you."

"It wasn't enough, though," she whispered. "If you hadn't come up..." She couldn't finish that thought.

And from the way his body shivered against hers, he couldn't either. "You fought back," he repeated.

"I fought back," she repeated, her words soft. "I'm still so sorry this ended up on your doorstep. It shouldn't have. He never should have come here and done this."

"We can agree on that part as long as you remember it wasn't your fault," he growled.

"I…I can do that."

She looked up at him then, her hand on his chest, the other on his arm, holding him steady. "I asked you to make me forget before, but now I don't think I can ever forget. Instead…instead, can you just make me *feel*? Help me remember what I can have with you rather than what happened earlier?"

He frowned, cupping her cheek softly. "You're hurt."

"Not really." He opened his mouth to argue, and she shook her head, silencing him for the moment. "You'll be careful. I know you will. You won't hurt me. But I want to finish our date, and I want tonight to be about *us*." Whatever *us* they happened to be.

"Kenzie…"

"Please."

He leaned down and kissed her lips. "You shouldn't have to beg, even with a simple word. I *want* you, Kenzie." And then he was finished speaking because his mouth was on hers, and she was falling into him once more.

He explored her mouth, and she moaned, needing his taste. She didn't want to think about what had happened earlier. All she wanted to do was remember what she and Dare had been doing before they walked into the inn and bar that night. They'd been on their date and getting closer and closer to going upstairs to make love.

No, not make love, have sex. She couldn't put emotions into what was going on where there couldn't be. Then Dare slid his hand up her back and down her hip, and she put all thoughts of what this what and what they could be out of her mind.

Live for the moment, she reminded herself. That was what she'd promised, and that was what they'd do tonight.

"I don't want to hurt you," he whispered as his hand trailed over her arm. He touched her where David had held her tightly, but when she looked into Dare's eyes, she didn't flinch.

"You're not him."

His eyes narrowed. "That much I know." He kissed her cheek, then her jaw, then her lips, then down her neck and to her collarbone. Then he had her in his arms, carrying her up the stairs to his bedroom.

She wrapped her arms around his neck and let out a squeal as he moved. "You're going to drop me! I'm too heavy for you."

He snorted and kept going until they were right at the edge of the bed. "You're not heavy, Red." He set her down on her feet, her body sliding along his in an erotic caress as he kept her upright using the strength in his hands.

He kissed her softly, his body firm and hard against hers as he slowly stripped her out of her dress. She loved this dress, the green of it bright against her skin and the red of her hair. But now when she felt it along her skin and thought of wearing it again, she wasn't sure she could do it.

David had thrown her on the floor in this dress. Had pressed her against the wall and tried to hurt her. She'd fought back, but she wasn't sure she could ever wear the dress that Dare had first seen her in again.

"Come back to me," Dare whispered against her mouth, pulling her from her treacherous thoughts. His hand went to her back, his fingers deftly undoing the clasp of her bra. The lace fell from her chest, her breasts heavy with need. He leaned down and licked the tip of one nipple before blowing cool air over her. She gasped, her nipple hardening into a tight bud. He did the same to her other breast, and she pressed her thighs together, craving release.

Dare went to his knees in front of her, kissing down her body as he did so, a nibble along the bottoms of her breasts, the valley between them, her stomach, her hips, then a lick over the edge of her thong.

She sucked in a breath and reached out to run her hands over his short crop of hair. "Dare."

"I need to taste you." He slowly slid her panties down her hips, kissing her thighs and the little indentions above her mound. She stepped out of her thong with his help, then let out a shocked breath as he kissed her pussy, his tongue sliding between her folds.

He sucked and licked at her clit, using his fingers to spread her for his gaze and his mouth. All the while, she kept her hand on his head, the vision of his dark hair between her thighs almost too much. Soon, her knees went weak, and Dare had his hands on her ass, keeping her upright as he made her come on his tongue.

Before she could honestly catch her breath and formulate any sense of words, Dare had her on her side in the middle of the bed and had stripped his clothes. He stood behind her, rolling a condom over his length as she looked over her shoulder.

"This way?" she asked, her voice breathy with anticipation.

"This way," he said, sliding onto the bed behind her. He positioned himself between her legs, her butt pressed against his hips as he pulled one of her legs slightly up. Then he had his mouth on hers and was sliding into her wet heat at the same moment. She gasped, sucking on his tongue and he pumped slow strokes in and out of her.

"You're so deep like this," she said softly.

"Want me deeper?" he asked, his voice low, a growl.

"That's possible?" she asked, licking her lips, then his bottom one.

In answer, he lowered her leg so her thighs touched, all the while thrusting in and out of her. "You're so damned tight this way," he growled. "I'm going to blow soon if I'm not careful."

"I...I...this feels so good."

"Good." He kept moving, her arching against him as he slid in and out of her with slow, demanding strokes. Despite how good it felt, she couldn't come this way, not tonight. Oh, she might be able to orgasm, and with Dare, she knew she'd come hard, but she needed to see his eyes.

"I need to see you," she said quickly, her breath coming in pants. "I want to see you, face you. I don't want to come yet."

He was so quiet that she thought she'd made a mistake, been too honest and had bared herself when she shouldn't have. But then he pulled out of her fully and turned her around so she was facing him. When he cupped her face and kissed her, a single tear slid down her cheek. She hoped he hadn't seen, but when he kissed that tear away, she lifted her leg slightly, and he slid in again.

They were patient with each other, moving together until her breasts ached and her inner walls clenched around him. She came while kissing him so she wouldn't say anything she couldn't take back, and his grip tightened on her as his body jerked, his release breathtaking.

They lay there, their bodies entwined, not speaking. She wasn't sure what she *could* say. Dare had been there for her when she needed him most, and now she was afraid that she'd made yet one more mistake in her long line of them.

She might have just fallen for the wrong man.

Again.

13

I T HAD BEEN two days since Kenzie realized she'd done the unthinkable and started to fall in love with Dare Collins. And in those two days, she'd done nothing but bury herself in work and try to forget that fact.

They had gone into their relationship with no promises other than that there would *be* no promises.

And her heart had decided to make a mockery of her.

It had also been two days since David was arrested and then subsequently let out on bail. She fisted her hands under her desk in the inn hallway and told herself that everything had to be okay. Just because her ex-husband had somehow found a loophole to get himself out of jail on his good behavior and standing didn't mean anything would come of it.

Apparently, he and his team of lawyers had told the judge that she was the one who instigated it, and he'd only been defending himself. It had been a load of bull since all evidence proved that he had been the one to show up at her place of business, unannounced, and had hurt her—far more than she had him. That she'd been able to knee the man in the balls at all to try and get away was something she could be proud of later, she supposed, but he'd tried to use that against her.

It hadn't worked as of yet since the charges of aggravated

assault hadn't been dropped, but according to the smirk on David's face at the bail hearing, he didn't think anything he'd done was too serious.

Not that she'd been in the courtroom for that. Thankfully, the lawyer Dare had helped her find was able to do the initial things without her there and had told her about that not so hidden smirk. Oh, David might have hidden it from the judge and those who could hurt him, but he hadn't hidden it from her lawyer. The bastard had wanted her to know that he wasn't the least remorseful for what he'd done.

And while she couldn't quite breathe when she thought about what could have happened and what could *still* happen, she knew she couldn't let her fear run her life. That was what she'd promised herself when she left him, and that was how she would lead her life now.

But she'd be aware.

No matter what.

So she pushed her fear out of her mind and went about her business. She could bury herself in her work, in her growing friendship with Ainsley, and…Dare.

Dare.

How had she ended up in this situation? She hadn't meant to find a man, let alone allow it to become anything more than a fling. But she knew they were growing serious even if neither of them wanted to admit it. Of course, that could all be a lie she told herself. He could want nothing more from her than what they had in bed. Dare might only be as protective as he was toward her because that was just who he was.

He protected those in his care, even if he might not truly *care* about them the way others might see it.

"You look like you're thinking really hard over there."

Kenzie's head shot up as Ainsley moved toward her. "Oh, sorry. I just…" She didn't know what she was going to say, so she trailed off. Ainsley gave her a knowing look before reaching out and patting Kenzie's hand gently.

"Are you almost done for the day? I figured we could try that other flight this evening. Or maybe just some wine? Dare's working in the restaurant tonight, but Rick is bartending, and I can see if Loch and Fox are around to hang out with us."

"Are you trying to make sure I'm never alone?"

"Maybe." Ainsley shrugged. "If, you know, that's what you want."

This was just one more reason she was glad she'd moved to Whiskey. These people *cared* about her even if she wasn't sure she knew how to care for them back.

Kenzie looked down at her desk and closed the notebook she'd been writing in before she went down the rabbit hole of her mind. "I think whiskey sounds pretty good."

"Yay!" Ainsley clapped her hands like a cheerleader, making them both laugh—something Kenzie sorely needed.

She came around the desk, and the two of them linked arms before walking down the main stairs. Kenzie came up short when she saw a familiar dark-haired woman with a soft smile on her face.

"Jesse," Kenzie said slowly. "Were you looking for Dare?"

The other woman shook her head, and Ainsley let go of Kenzie's arm. "Hey, Jesse, it's good to see you."

Jesse smiled at Ainsley, bringing the other woman into a hard hug. "Hey, honey. Do you mind if I steal your girl for a bit? I won't be long."

Kenzie stiffened but gave Ainsley a nod when her friend glanced over at her.

"I'll just go find Loch since he's been his normal butthead self," Ainsley said with a shrug. "Give me a call if you need me." She gave Kenzie a quick hug before letting herself out of the front entryway.

That left Ainsley standing on the bottom stair slightly above Jesse. "So…"

Jesse let out a laugh. "This got way more secretive and *important* than I planned on. I just wanted to see if you were okay after the attack and talk to you a bit about something that's been on my mind. It's not scary or anything."

Kenzie relaxed at that, even though her stomach ached at the thought of talking about the attack again. But it wasn't like she could hide from it. Whiskey was a small town, and everyone knew what had happened. And though Jesse didn't live in Whiskey, she was still close enough to those who lived inside the town borders to have heard things.

"Do you want to come upstairs to my room? Or we can go into the bar. It's not that busy yet I don't think."

"I spotted our booth empty in the corner."

"Sounds like a plan," Kenzie said as she followed the other woman to the bar. Soon, they were sitting together, talking about nothing important with a glass of wine in front of each of them. She hadn't spotted Dare yet, and she wasn't sure what this was about, but for some reason, she knew it was important.

So many things seemed important these days, and she wasn't sure what to make of it.

"Dare told you about his time before he owned this place?" Jesse asked. She'd made it sound like a question, but from the look in the other woman's eyes, Kenzie knew that Jesse probably already knew the answer.

Kenzie looked down at the wine glass in her hand and nodded. "Yes. He told me." She met the other woman's gaze, hoping she could say the right thing. "I am so sorry about Jason. I don't know what I'd do if…" She shook her head, words seeming a bit useless right then. "I just don't know what I'd do."

Jesse gave her a sad smile. "I didn't know what I'd do either. They tell you to be prepared when you marry a cop. Hell, they tell you to be prepared when you marry anyone in a position where their life is on the line protecting those they love…and those they've never met. But being a cop was what Jason loved to do. He was good at it. He loved me, and loved the baby growing inside of me. He was one of those guys that could put away the job when he came home. He'd talk to me if he needed to, and he'd talk to his brothers, as well. He never wanted to be the one who bottled it all up inside and ended up hurting himself in the process. I don't know how he became so self-aware, but that was my husband. And I miss him every damn moment of every damn day, even if my heart is scabbed over, I still feel that wound."

Kenzie was quiet, listening to the other woman speak. How Jesse could even sit here and talk about her husband without breaking down, she didn't know, but Kenzie sure as hell admired her strength and the depth of her love for the man she'd lost.

"Dare isn't like Jason," Jesse said, bringing Kenzie from her thoughts.

She swallowed hard. "What do you mean?"

"Jason did his best to bring Dare out of his shell and open up about what they were going through even when it was smaller cases that didn't end in shouting or an arrest. Dare was a great cop. Hard-working and efficient. He put his all into it, and yet he internalized everything. He smiled more than he does now, he laughed and joked with his family and did everything he could for them. He still does the latter, honestly, which I guess you can see just by watching him interact with them. But he's not the same man he was before the shooting." She paused. "I don't think any of us are the same people as before, and I honestly don't know if anyone *could* be the same after something like that."

"I don't think so either." Kenzie met Jesse's gaze. "He doesn't sleep. I mean, he does when he's exhausted, and between work and everything else, he's tired more than ever, but he still dreams." She paused, not sure why she was telling Jesse this but knowing she had to. "I don't know how to help him. He does so much to help me even though I don't want to need the help, but I don't know how to help him."

Jesse reached out and gripped her hand. "Don't stop trying. I don't know what the two of you are to each other, nor do I know what you two say you want, but don't stop trying. He needs you, even if he won't say it. When you're with him, I see the man he could be. And I know that's a heavy weight to put on your shoulders. I'm sorry for that, but don't give up, Kenzie. He's such an amazing man, and I want him to see that. I think you could do that for him."

Kenzie opened her mouth to say something, but before she could, a familiar sense of awareness spread over her. She turned as Dare walked toward them, concern on his face for a moment before he schooled his features into a smile.

"There're my girls," he said before leaning down to kiss her cheek then doing the same to Jesse. "Doing okay tonight?"

"Just hanging with your girl," Jesse said on a laugh. "Now I need to go and pick up my baby from my parents. It was good talking to you, Kenzie." She stood up and kissed Dare's cheek. "Don't do anything I wouldn't do." And with that, she walked away, leaving Kenzie and Dare alone at her corner booth.

"Hey," he said, stuffing his hands into his pockets.

Kenzie looked up at him, her heart beating in her chest. "Hey there."

"So, I need to close for the night but once I'm done, want me to come up?"

She licked her lips and got out of the booth so she could stand in front of him. He immediately put his hands on her hips and brought his head down for a kiss. She didn't moan, but she was sure as heck close just from his touch alone. This man did things to her that made her crazy.

"I'm going to finish my glass of wine and head upstairs to eat what I have in the fridge. But when you're done working? I'd love for you to come upstairs."

He nodded, a smile playing over his lips. "My goal is for you to come, too, you know."

She rolled her eyes even as laughter bubbled up her throat. "I walked into that one, didn't I?"

"Pretty much." He paused. "You and Jesse okay?"

Kenzie nodded, even though she was still digesting how the conversation had gone. "We were just having girl time. She's a nice woman."

He smiled fully then, and her heart warmed. "Yeah, she is. I'm glad she has someone to talk to that isn't her parents or kid, you know?"

She wasn't sure he'd like it as much if he knew where their conversation had gone, but that wasn't something she was going to get into at the moment.

She went up on her toes and kissed his chin, knowing she couldn't bite it like she wanted to with so many people around. "Upstairs soon?"

He growled low. "Soon."

She sauntered away, moving her hips with just enough sway that she knew his eyes were glued to her butt. Because if she worked hard at it, she knew they could focus on the heat between them, the chemistry, and not the percolating feelings and issues that kept creeping up.

She didn't want to want him with the intensity she did, and she knew he felt the same way. At least, that's what he'd told her at first. They couldn't go and change the game at this point.

It wouldn't be fair to either of them. Not when she didn't know what she wanted. So she'd pretend that everything was just heat between them. Heat with a touch of…something else.

It was either that or go mad. And she'd almost done that before; she refused to do it again.

She hoped.

14

"YOU SOUND HAPPY," Dare said into the phone as he leaned back against the wall in the dining room on his way back from the kitchen. He had a beer in his hand with his family in the living room close by, and he was doing his best to keep his tone light no matter what they talked about.

Tabby laughed into the phone. "I *am* happy." She paused, and he knew she was thinking about what exactly made her this happy. "I never thought this would happen, you know? I never thought I'd find someone who's my other half in so many ways. We're so different, yet when it comes down to it, those differences make us work." She laughed again, and Dare couldn't help but smile. His baby sister needed to laugh, and that Montgomery she was about to marry knew how to make her do it.

"Well, if Alex ever stops making you laugh like that, I'll come down and kick his ass."

"First, big brother, if he stops making me laugh, *I'll* kick his ass. It's what we do. He taught me how to fight and protect myself, so I'll take him down." There was laughter in her voice as she said that, but he had a feeling she wasn't necessarily joking. Alex had trained her in self-defense, and Dare knew Loch had flown out there to give her pointers as well after she was hurt in an attack. They all blamed themselves for not making sure she was safe, even hundreds of miles away.

"Okay, stop grumbling over there," Tabby warned. "I'm done with all of you being all overprotective."

He hadn't even said anything, but apparently, his silence was enough. "I'm glad you're happy, Tabs. And we'll be out there for the wedding with no problems. I made sure the staff here is aware, so just do what you need to do, and we'll be there."

"We? Are you bringing Kenzie?"

Dare sputtered. "Uh, I was actually talking about Nate since Monica is letting me have him for the wedding." That had been a chore in itself, but he wasn't about to get into that with Tabby or any of his family for that matter. "Kenzie and I aren't...well, I don't think we're at a wedding stage yet." His stomach tightened, and he coughed. "I mean taking each other to weddings yet. Like across the country and shit."

"So eloquent, Dare. Good to know you're comfortable enough in your relationship not to stutter and sound like you're having a panic attack when you talk about a trip together."

Dare pinched the bridge of his nose, aware that his parents and brothers were now staring at him from the living room. Well, great, at least his audience would be entertained while he tried to get his foot out of his mouth. Thankfully, Nate and Kenzie weren't there, or he'd need to find a deck to jump off or something.

"You caught me off guard. And now I'm going to go because Fox is glaring at me, and I'm pretty sure Loch is going to pound me if I don't get off the phone and explain to them that I'm not an asshole."

"You're still an asshole," Fox called out.

"Dude, Misty is napping," Loch griped. "She's getting over

her cold, so don't wake her up." He punched Fox in the arm, and the two of then snorted at each other.

"Tell them I miss them and will call them soon," Tabby said. "And maybe you should, you know, think about your relationship with Kenzie if it's been going on for more than a couple of nights. Besides, I hear you two are practically sleeping at each other's places every night."

"Bye, Tabs. Love you." He hung up before she could pester him again and ignored the looks his parents gave him. They liked Kenzie as their innkeeper, and from the way his mother gushed about her, they wanted her to be a part of the group as more than just a friend.

They *loved* the idea of the two of them dating, and that worried him. Sure, he'd been slightly worried about what his parents would think about him sleeping with the innkeeper—especially since he'd been an asshole to her that first morning—but now he was worried they liked the idea too much.

He and Kenzie weren't serious.

And that was a fucking lie, and they both knew it.

He didn't know what they were going to do about it, but hell, he needed to think long and hard before he fucked things up for her and him...and his kid, for that matter.

"Tabby okay?" his mom called out, and he stuffed his phone into his pocket so he could walk into the living room.

"Yeah, I thought you talked to her like daily." He sat down next to Loch, who shifted over slightly, giving him more room.

"Of course, I do, but I wanted to make sure things hadn't changed since this morning. And we talk so much more often now with the wedding. I'm talking to Alex's mother almost daily now too, even though we aren't the ones planning it. Tabby and

Alex are doing everything themselves, and since my baby girl is such a planner, she's loving it. They're going small, which makes them happy, and I'm just glad we're all going to be able to go down there together as a family." She narrowed her eyes. "Monica is letting you bring Nate? My grandson had better be able to see his aunt get married because she doesn't get to know him as it is. *I* don't get to know my grandson enough."

Loch mumbled under his breath, and from his chair, Fox winced. When their mom went on a tear about Monica, things got ugly. Dare didn't mind a little complaining since, hell, he missed his kid, too, but he got tired if it went on too long.

"You see him once a month, and you get to talk to him often. Soon, he'll be doing school events and things, and we're all allowed to go to those. Stop griping on Monica, Mom, okay? She's great with Nate."

"I'm not saying she isn't. But a boy needs his father."

He set his beer down, no longer in the mood. "He has a father."

"I'm not talking about his stepfather," his mother snapped before sighing. "I didn't mean that. I'm sorry."

"I know you didn't," he said through gritted teeth. "Auggie's not bad." That was as much leeway as he'd give the man that was allowed more time with Nate than he had. "But, yeah, Mom, Nate is coming with me for the wedding. Special events like that are built into to the custody agreement."

"You need a new custody agreement," she said quickly. "Because this isn't working, baby. I want you happy. And now that you're with Kenzie—"

He held up his hand, cutting her off. "Don't bring her up when you mention custody or my kid, okay?"

"Dare," his mother chided.

"Don't. Just don't. Stay out of my relationship with Kenzie. We're still new, and the idea that you think any judge is going to want to change things custody-wise, or that Monica is going to let me have more time with my son because everyone thinks I have a girlfriend is crazy. Don't mix up the two things I have going on in my life." Not yet, anyway. His brain was doing that enough for everyone.

"You're mixing up everything I'm trying to say, Dare."

"That's enough, Barb," his father put in. "Let the boy figure out what he's doing before you try to fix it. There's nothing to fix if he's still working it out."

And that was one reason he and his father got along so well; his dad understood that Dare was constantly thinking and trying to compartmentalize and yet, sometimes, he couldn't figure out how to do that until he sat back and untangled all the threads.

"I need to go," he said. "I told Nate I'd call him, and I have work to do."

"I should head out, too," Fox said. "I have work to do, and I'm behind on making sure my ads guy is keeping up with his shit."

Loch stood up, cleaning up their single beer bottles that none of them had finished. "I'll stay until Misty wakes from her nap, then we need to leave also."

"Now, stop it, all three of you. I wasn't trying to push you out of our house." His mother bit her lip, and Dare couldn't help but lean down and kiss the top of her head.

"We really do have to go, Mom. You didn't do anything wrong. You just want to fix things that I'm not sure I have the capacity to fix yet. Okay? Just let me be for a bit."

"You know I love you."

He smiled, this time knowing it reached his eyes. "I know."

"And I worry."

He couldn't help the laugh that escaped. "That I know, too."

And with that, they said their goodbyes, and he headed back to his place. While he enjoyed their family dinners, he knew that sometimes they took energy from him that he needed for other things.

Namely, figuring out what the hell he was going to do about Kenzie.

"Jesus," he muttered to himself. How the hell had this happened? He'd been fine before she walked into his bar. He hadn't needed to think about anything except his kid, his family, and his job. Sure, he'd go home with a woman every once in a while, but more often than not, he'd go to bed after tasting one of his whiskeys.

Alone.

That had all changed once he got to know Kenzie just a little bit. He hadn't been able to get her out of his mind, nor had he been able to make the right decisions when it came to her. He should have stayed away. He never should have gotten close.

But if he hadn't...he could have lost her.

He parked in front of his house and gripped his steering wheel. He could have lost her because that asshole David had gotten too close. He'd hurt her, and Dare had almost been too late to do anything except pull the steaming pile of shit off her.

He couldn't even let the thought of what could have happened if he hadn't been there enter his mind. If he did...well, he might just break his steering wheel off completely. And because he knew he needed to cool down, he went inside his house, didn't bother to turn on the lights, and sank into the big chair in his living room. He needed to think, and he wasn't sure he was going to like where his thoughts ended up.

Kenzie was so much better than either of the two men in her life, past or present. She was funny, smart, and had so much in front of her whether she stayed at the Whiskey Inn or moved on to something bigger once she healed from her divorce. He knew if he let himself, he'd fall for her, hard. He was doing his best not to acknowledge the fact that he might have already done so.

He wasn't the man for her. They'd both known that going in, hadn't they? She'd needed to use him to heal, and he'd needed to use her to feel. That was all they needed. They'd known it would be temporary. They couldn't do anything more than that because that wasn't what they'd agreed on.

And if he kept telling himself that, maybe it would be true.

The doorbell rang, and he frowned then cursed when he remembered that Kenzie was supposed to come by after handing over the reins to the night shift.

Fuck.

He wasn't in any state to see her, not when his head wasn't on straight, but he couldn't just leave her outside, waiting, either. He wasn't that much of an asshole.

When he opened the door, she stood on the other side, a small bag in her hand. Neither of them had been brave or ready enough to leave things at each other's houses. They'd only been together for a few weeks, and they were doing their damndest not to talk about the state of their relationship.

They were making so many fucking mistakes by not just talking to each other about what they wanted. But since he didn't know what that was, maybe it was the best thing he *could* do.

"Hey," he said, taking a step back so she could walk in. "You look nice."

She smiled and looked down at her normal work skirt and top. "Thanks. You saw me in this earlier when you stopped by to work on paperwork with Claire."

He shrugged and leaned forward to kiss her. It was meant to be a soft brush of lips, but at the first taste of her, he couldn't stop the moan that escaped. They were both breathless by the time he pulled away and took her bag with him, gently sliding the strap from her shoulder.

"You still look good."

"Well, if that's how you're going to greet me after I wear the same outfit for ten hours, I might just have to do it again."

Again. Because they were going to see each other again like this. Because this wasn't just a fling. This was something more.

And damned if he knew what to do about it other than keep going and try not to fuck it up.

His phone buzzed in his pocket as they made their way into the living room, and he pulled it out, frowning. "It's Monica."

Kenzie's eyes widened. "I hope Nate's okay."

He did, too, but the fact that Kenzie's first thought was about Nate did something to his chest. "Monica? What's wrong? Is Nate okay?" Dare didn't usually call for a couple of hours, so it was weird to have her call *him*.

"He's fine. Sorry to call now and worry you, but I wanted to talk to you when Nate wasn't in the room."

Shit. "I'm glad he's fine," he said more for Kenzie's benefit than Monica's. When Kenzie immediately relaxed, he knew he was once again in dangerous territory when it came to his innkeeper.

"What's up?"

"I know you're supposed to have Nate next weekend, but can we switch? Auggie has a family event coming up, and Nate needs to be there."

No the fuck he didn't.

"Excuse me?"

"It's a family picnic for his work, Dare." She sighed, and he knew she was about to talk to him like he was a damn twelve-year-old instead of the father of her son. This was one more reason why he'd never married her. She might be a good woman and a better mom, but they didn't fit. Never had, and he had been too dense and focused on his job to notice that earlier.

"AUGGIE NEEDS US to be there. Everyone is bringing their children, and it is a great way for the higher-ups to bond."

"Auggie isn't Nate's dad," he growled out.

"Jesus, Dare. Get a grip." She started to rant, and Dare pinched the bridge of his nose.

Kenzie gave him a worried look and went to the fridge, pulling out two beers. When she handed it to him, he gave her a nod, thankful that she wasn't saying anything since his relationship with Kenzie wasn't a conversation he really wanted to have with Monica just yet. Yeah, his ex knew about Kenzie in theory, but when even he wasn't sure what they were to each other, adding complications to the mix would only make things harder for everyone. At least, for now.

"You know, Monica, I would have been fine changing weekends if you'd have given me a heads-up earlier. Hell, you know I want any time I can with Nate. But two days before I'm supposed to *finally* have time with my son? I don't fucking think so. This picnic sounds like it's been a thing for a while now, and you're just *now* telling me? That's not my problem."

"Nate."

"No, I'm not done. You're not changing our Christmas plans either. You're not taking him away from me because you need to make your husband look good."

"Why is everything a fight with you? I'm letting you take *my* son all the way to freaking Colorado, and I didn't put up a fuss."

"First, he's *our* son. I've been there since the beginning. I didn't walk out on you, Monica. You walked out on me. Don't put this all on me."

Monica made a loud growl that sounded more like a screech, and he knew she was trying to keep from saying something they'd both regret. She'd done it when they were dating, and it had always annoyed him. Now? He knew it was the only way she could keep her temper in check.

"We're not getting anything figured out right now. We keep coming up to this wall where you want more time with him, and I don't want to end up hurting either of you when I'm figuring things out. So why don't we talk when I pick up him after your weekend. Or something." She paused. "I don't know how to continue what we're doing, Dare, because I don't want to hate you, but fighting over weekends is making me act like someone I'm not."

He frowned. "So you don't want to change my weekend, after all? Is that so you can have Christmas?" He cursed inwardly at his sharp tone. "Shit. I didn't mean that to sound so accusatory."

"I know you didn't, and because we're fighting all the time

over *Nate's* time we're….we're not doing good. We need to talk. Soon. Because this isn't working."

Dare's blood went cold at her words, and he knew if he wasn't careful, he might just lose everything he had.

"We'll talk when you pick him up." He did his best to keep his voice casual. Light. Because if he said something that pissed her off, it could ruin everything.

She hung up after saying goodbye, and he looked down at his phone, his mind going in a thousand different directions but none of them making any sense to him at all.

"Dare? What's wrong?"

"I…I have no idea." He met her gaze, and she leaned over the counter to grip his free hand.

"What can I do?"

And that was the thing. He didn't know. He didn't know what was going to happen when he talked to Monica, and having Kenzie here when he felt so…off just reminded him that he didn't know what he was doing when it came to her either.

His paths were coming to an intersection, and if he weren't careful, he could lose everything—things he hadn't even known he wanted.

And because he had no idea what to do, he let his thoughts go to the back of his mind and focused on what was in front of him. Putting down his phone, he leaned forward and kissed Kenzie softly, the island between them making it hard for him to touch her but that distance was needed.

"You're doing it," he finally answered as he pulled away. "You're here." And though that might just be the problem, he didn't push her away.

Instead, he walked around the counter and held her close,

knowing after everything that had happened recently, sometimes words weren't useful and falling into each other was the only thing you could do. Because Dare had fallen for Kenzie. There was no denying the heavy feeling in his chest anymore.

He'd fallen for her when he promised himself he wouldn't. He was no good for her. She deserved far better, but now, he wasn't sure he could go back.

He just hoped he wasn't making yet another mistake.

Because the last time he'd done that, he'd lost Jason.

And everything else around him.

15

NATE ROLLED ON the grass in front of him, giggling like mad as Kenzie took a photo with her phone. She smiled, laughing with him, and his son just ate it up. Dare leaned back against the porch railing, watching them both as he tried not to imagine what this could be like in a few years if he still had Kenzie in his life.

They'd made love all night and into the morning after he figured out what that twist in his heart meant. And then he'd done his best not to think about it—something he was getting far too good at when it came to the important things in his life. They'd both worked and spent time together and acted as if they hadn't crossed an invisible line into who they were now as a couple rather than who they'd told themselves they'd be. There wasn't anything casual about them, and from the long looks they gave one another, they both knew it.

He wanted to tell her he loved her, wanted to shout it to the world, but at the same time, he wanted to let it settle over him just a bit longer. He hadn't known what this emotion felt like for someone other than his family before, and he was worried he was going to screw everything up. And he had a feeling if he let himself just *be*, he might lose her. She still wasn't fully out of her ex's clutches, and Dare would be damned if he let his feelings confuse or hurt her any more than she already was.

But before he could let his thoughts once again go down a path that made his head hurt, his phone buzzed. The readout was a familiar number that shocked his system every time he saw it, though it had been a long time since he had.

"This is Collins." He answered the way he had on the force, and his tone must have caught Kenzie's ear. She gave him a questioning look, and he shook his head, motioning over to Nate, who was still rolling around and giggling like mad. She nodded over at Dare before going to play with his son, and for that, he was grateful.

"Dare, good to hear your voice, man," one of his former colleagues said. "Damn good to hear your voice."

"You too, Steve." And that was true enough. While Dare missed those he'd worked with in the past, he liked his new life and job even more than he had being a cop. Some jobs weren't for everyone, and while he valued his time on the force, and was grateful for the paths he'd taken, he was content—perhaps *more* than content—with his life now.

Huh, interesting.

"So, anyway, I just wanted to give you an update on those letters you dropped off." Dare stiffened, his jaw clenching, thinking of Jesse and her daughter.

"What do you know?"

"We looked into the kid and his family, and while the boy definitely needs to talk to someone, it wasn't malicious. We didn't see any true intent to do harm. The mother is sending the kid to a new therapist and wants to ensure you that she's going to do everything she can to get him the help he needs." Steve let out a breath. "Honestly, Dare, it looks like a kid who's hurting and doesn't know who to lash out at with his feelings, but he has no intent to do so with his fists or anything physical. He broke down into tears, man."

"He wrote Jesse, Steve. I don't care if that kid cried." That was a lie, but he still wasn't ready to forgive.

"I know, man. And we took it seriously. From what we could tell, once we talked to the kid, he took it seriously, too. We're not done watching him because, fuck, you don't mess with one of us or our families, but we really don't think this kid means you harm."

Dare sighed, slightly relieved but still worried. "That's good to hear but…"

"But we're not letting it go completely, don't worry. We're not going to let anything slip through because we *want* to think the kid is safe."

He talked to Steve a bit longer, his head not really into catching up with people that were no longer in his life, not when he was looking at the way Kenzie and Nate laughed with one another.

He hadn't meant for them to get so close and interact like they were, but he hadn't been able to keep them apart. Not when he wanted to spend time with both of them. Nate had started asking questions about Kenzie, not anything serious, but more like questions about whether he was going to see her over the weekend. Dare knew that he'd have to be careful as time went on so he wouldn't end up hurting his son, but he also knew he couldn't keep them apart when he had Nate. He wanted to spend time with Kenzie, and Nate did too, so that meant the three of them were on this precarious path where he hoped he was making the right decisions.

The thing was, he kept thinking about the fact that when Monica came soon to pick up Nate, she'd said she wanted to talk with him about why they were fighting all the time about custody. Dare didn't want to argue, but he was damn tired of missing out on the important things when it came to his son.

He had a stable job and a good team who could take over the day-to-day things if he needed time off to be more flexible for Nate. Dare also had a strong family that could help at the drop of a hat, each of his brothers and parents being pillars in the community—even if Fox and Loch would scoff at that.

He wanted more time with Nate, and he hoped to hell Monica would make that happen. But a small part of him was worried that Monica wanted to change things for the worse. At least for him. What if she wanted Nate to never have holidays or weekends with him? What if she made sure the courts saw that he still worked in a bar and wasn't settled down or married yet as points against him?

What if they thought his past life as a cop could come back and bite him in the ass as it almost had with those letters?

What if they figured that Dare dating and not in a serious relationship would be too hard on Nate and they took him away?

He let out a breath, pissed off with himself for letting his mind go down that path. He didn't know exactly what Monica wanted to talk about and he needed to go in with no preconceived notions that could possibly trigger his temper and screw everything up.

Kenzie walked up to him at that instant, Nate by her side, and Dare pushed all of those thoughts out of his mind. He'd promised Kenzie that he'd live in the now since that was what she was trying to do, but he couldn't quite help where his mind went when it came to his son.

"Did you find the leaves you wanted?" Dare asked, running a hand through Nate's soft hair.

His kid beamed up at him. "Yeah. Can I keep them here with my rock?"

Dare held back a wince at that. He'd kept the smooth rock for his son, but leaves in the house? That might be going too far. "How about we keep them on the porch in one of those stone bowls Grandma brought over? That way, they can be near their leaf brothers."

Kenzie shot him a look at his bullshit, and he did his best not to laugh. Kids, man, they made you say the weirdest shit.

"Okay!" Nate jumped up and down before running to carefully set his leaves in one of the stone bowls.

Kenzie leaned into Dare's side, and he wrapped an arm around her shoulders and placed a quick kiss on her temple before Nate turned back. And because he had his attention on his kid and Kenzie, he missed the sound of Monica's car pulling up. He'd apparently lost all his cop senses since becoming a civilian.

"Hey," Monica said, smiling over at Nate before giving Kenzie and Dare a look.

Dare pulled away from Kenzie only to turn and face his ex. "Didn't hear you come up, were you waiting long?"

She shook her head. "I heard you back here, so I just walked around back instead of ringing the doorbell."

He nodded and cleared his throat. "Monica, this is Kenzie, Kenzie, this is Monica, Nate's mom." See? Civil, and not at all awkward. Kenzie was the first woman he'd really dated since Monica, so he'd never had to introduce anyone to Nate or his ex before. He hoped he was doing it right. Wasn't there a handbook or something for this?

"Nice to meet you," Kenzie said, holding out her hand.

Monica shook it, and he could tell his ex was studying Kenzie, but not in a malicious way. Just in the way two people did when they met and were connected through other people in their lives.

"Nice to meet you, too." Monica looked over at Dare. "Think we can talk for a minute?"

He nodded. "Mind watching Nate for a few?" he asked Kenzie.

"No problem," she said, looking between the two of them.

"Mommy!" Nate cried out, running toward them. He flung himself into Monica's open arms with the exuberance of any small child hyped up on playing—and a teeny amount of sugar.

"Hey, pumpkin, your dad and I are going to talk for a minute, but Daddy's friend, Kenzie, is going to hang out with you for a bit. Is that okay?"

Nate grinned and wrapped his arms around Kenzie's middle. "Uh-huh. I like Kenzie."

Kenzie smiled softly. "I like you, too, kiddo."

Dare ran his hand over Nate's head again, met Kenzie's eyes, and blew out a breath. See? They were doing this, and no one was yelling or freaking out. Maybe everything would be okay, and he could figure out exactly how he'd take the next steps—whatever they might be.

He and Monica walked off to the side of the house while Kenzie went to ensure that Nate's leaves were safely in their bowl.

"So..." Dare began, not sure what to say, or what Monica

had planned.

"I'm tired of fighting, Dare." She looked off into the distance at the large trees he had behind his house and held back a sigh.

"I'm not fond of it either, Mon."

"When I left, it wasn't because I didn't want you in Nate's life."

Dare set his jaw but didn't say anything. She had a lead-up, and that was just how she got into heavy subjects. He'd taught himself long ago not to interrupt her, or they'd go off track and start yelling. Again, he didn't hate Monica, but it wasn't always the easiest thing *not* to fight with her either.

"We weren't working together, and that was something we both knew. I'm not putting words into your mouth because you said something similar right at the end. You're an amazing father, Dare, but we weren't amazing together."

He kept silent, waiting for where she was going with this.

"When I filed for custody, it was because of the man you were when I left. The man I thought you were, for that matter." She met his gaze, and he did his best to keep the anger out of his eyes. "You loved your job so damn much, Dare. You put all your energy into it, your family, and honestly, just having a good time. We were young enough that the latter wasn't a bad thing, but I didn't know the father you'd be, and I didn't know if you were going to go back to being a cop once you figured out what you wanted. And because of that, I wanted to make sure Nate had the best life."

"A life without me in it," he bit out.

She raised her chin. "A *stable* life. That's all I wanted. I never wanted to take him out of your life completely, but I also didn't want him to get hurt."

"I'd never hurt Nate, and I resent you using that excuse to keep him away from me. I hate that I'm missing everything because I only get him for forty-eight hours out of a month. And I damn well resent the fact that you keep wanting to change my time with him because you want to help Auggie at work. That's pissing me off, Mon."

She nodded, her mouth pinched. "Yes, I know. And that's why things need to change."

Dare growled. "You're not taking him away from me. I'll fight."

Monica ran a hand over her face. "I know you will, but I'm not saying the change needs to be what you're thinking, Dare. Let me finish."

"Then talk faster because I'm not patient."

"Jesus, I know you aren't. I don't know how Kenzie puts up with you." She held up her hand. "Sorry. I didn't mean to bring her up. She seems nice."

"She is, and she's not part of this conversation."

She raised a brow. "Uh, she might just be if she's in your life for long because if she's in *your* life, then she's in Nate's, and *that* is my business."

"She's not. We're not. I just..."

"You'd better think about who she is to you if you want her around my kid, Dare. She's probably really sweet and nice to him, but I won't have Nate confused. And now I'm on a tangent." She blew out a breath. "I think it's time, now that he's older, that maybe we should talk about going more towards shared custody."

Dare blinked, surprised as hell. "What?"

"You're not the man I left and, frankly, I'm not the woman

who left you. I'm tired of fighting, and I think Nate needs both of us. Equally. So maybe we can talk about changing things up, but only if it's good for Nate."

Dare could barely process what she was telling him. He couldn't quite formulate the words as his mind went in a thousand different directions and warmth spread through him.

"You'd let me have him more often?" he asked, his voice hoarse.

"If we can work things out? I hope so. But, Dare, I don't want Nate hurt. And that means you need to think about what you want and what's best for him before we sign papers or go over things. Okay?"

He *knew* she was talking about Kenzie but hadn't wanted to use her name and start a fight. And since he wasn't sure where he and Kenzie were, he kept his mouth shut and tried to make his brain catch up with what was going on in front of him.

He had a chance to get more time with his son. After all this time, he might actually get everything he'd ever wanted. His kid, his job, and his family were all coming together and making his world…better.

But with all of that, he knew he had to think long and hard about what it meant for him and Kenzie. Because he didn't know where they were at in their relationship or how serious they could be…how serious they were.

And if Monica decided that she wouldn't budge because he was with Kenzie? He wasn't sure what he could do other than fight.

And that meant he had to talk to Kenzie and see how she felt. Because while part of him knew she was worth fighting for, the other part was worried that she didn't want to fight at all.

Yet, no matter what, he promised himself, he'd have to do right by his son.

Even if it broke Dare in the process.

16

THERE WAS SOMETHING off, and Kenzie knew it, but she couldn't quite figure out what it was. And because she was at the point where she was tired of keeping things in, she'd have to talk to Dare.

She was falling for him, or might have already done so, and though that broke their original agreement, she wasn't sure either one of them was in that place anymore.

But before she exposed her innermost feelings to him, she needed to figure out why he'd put just a little bit of distance between them after Monica left his house the day before. He hadn't told her what the two of them had talked about, and she wasn't going to ask, not when she knew it would just be prying at this point. If he wanted to talk about it with her, he would, but the fact that he hadn't worried her.

And not just because her name had probably been mentioned since she'd just met the mother of his child. Kenzie would have expected that, after all—and welcomed it. But, no, the fact that Dare didn't want to share or *couldn't* share made her think that maybe the slow progression of their relationship was all in her head and not really happening.

"I just need to talk to him," she mumbled to herself. It would be hard, she knew, but she needed to. Worrying about what she didn't know because she couldn't talk to him was useless and just a poor way to handle things. It wasn't necessarily a miscommunication, but it wasn't a good thing to do in any form of relationship.

So she'd talk to him. Tonight. No more worrying about what-ifs and figuring out exactly how she felt. Because there was no way she could accurately untangle her own feelings without knowing his.

She'd been stupid long enough.

Kenzie gasped as strong hands slid down her waist, over her skirt, and squeezed. "Dare," she whispered. "I'm working." And just thinking about him.

He moved her hair from her shoulder and kissed her neck. "Take a long lunch."

She didn't arch against him, but it was close. Anyone could walk by at any time, and she couldn't let them see what Dare did to her. That was only for them, no one else.

"Dare."

He bit gently down on her neck. "You don't have any guests right now, and didn't you say that you only have two check-ins, but both are later? They're only for the night, right? Play with me, Kenzie." There was almost a desperation in his tone, and while it should have worried her, she pushed it to the side of her mind and felt. Desperation led to more desperation.

"We'll have to be quick," she whispered, her breaths coming in pants. He pulled her away from the desk even as the last words left her mouth, tugging her toward the end of the hall. There were no guest rooms in this section, and her apartment was in the opposite direction, so she was slightly confused as to where he was taking her until he opened the door to the linen closet.

"Really? The closet?" She laughed as he tugged her inside and closed the door. He flipped on the light so they could see each other. He didn't answer her, though; instead, he held her close and crushed his mouth to hers. She arched into him, gripping his arms for a better hold as he backed her into the shelf on the other end of the closest. Sheets and pillows pressed into her back, and she smiled up at him once he moved away ever so slightly to catch his breath.

"I need to taste you," he growled.

She shook her head and pushed him slightly away from him. "Me first."

His eyes darkened. "You want my cock in that mouth of yours? Is that what you're saying? You want to suck me down and swallow my come?"

Her panties went wet at his words, and she licked her lips before going wordlessly to her knees. It wasn't easy in her tight skirt, but Dare held her hands so she wouldn't fall off her heels.

When she undid the button on his jeans, they both let out sharp breaths. She loved having Dare in her mouth, loved tasting him. No matter what they were going through or how many things happened around them that seemed to rattle their cages, the sex they shared was always mind-blowing. Sex wasn't their problem, and she knew it, but right then, all she wanted to do was suck Dare off and then have him come inside her.

She needed to cling to him for what felt like it would be the last time.

Why did that thought enter her mind? Why on *earth* did she think she'd never have him in her arms again after this moment?

Dare tugged on her hair, and she came back to the present

and out of the dark thoughts that kept creeping in, clinging to her sanity. He sent her a questioning look, and in answer, she unzipped his zipper and pulled his jeans down enough so she could grip his length. She loved the way he felt in her hand, thick and rigid. There was nothing soft about him right then, and she relished it.

At the first taste of him on her tongue, she hummed, pulling a groan out of Dare. She bobbed her head, sucking at the tip and using her hand to cup his balls, squeezing slightly.

He rocked back and forth, sliding between her lips as he tugged on her hair. She hollowed her cheeks, flicking her tongue down his shaft, loving the control she had over him. Oh, he might be the one with a hold on her hair, but she was the one making him lose it.

Dare pulled back suddenly on a growl and stood her up, taking her mouth with his in a demanding kiss. "I need you on my mouth, and if I come right now, I'm going to miss that sweet pussy of yours."

Understanding, she leaned back on the self, gripping the edge of it so she could widen her legs. Dare knelt in front of her and rucked her skirt up over her hips.

"I fucking love when you wear these tight skirts. It makes your ass look so fucking hot, and I know you're wet and ready for me underneath." He slid his knuckle over her damp panties, and she sucked in a breath. "You want my mouth on your pussy, baby? You want my tongue on your clit?"

In answer, she spread her legs wider.

"Fuck, yeah. You're already wet for me. He slowly slid her panties down her legs, but only to her knees. That meant her legs were restrained ever so slightly, but it only turned her on even more. With her butt resting on the shelf, she could easily sit and have him take control.

He gripped the bottom of her thighs and lowered his head, licking her pussy in one long swipe. She moaned, arching into him, keeping her grip tight on the shelf. He sucked and licked at her clit, humming and biting.

He teased her opening with his tongue before going back to her clit and sucking it into his mouth. With that, she came hard, biting her lip so she wouldn't call out his name or scream and let the world know what they were doing in the linen closet. Of course, with the moans and pants they were both making, anyone walking by this corner would know.

And for some reason, that turned her on even more.

She shouldn't feel like this, shouldn't feel so protected with him, yet she trusted him completely. She could let herself go in a way she'd never been able to with David and surely not in any way she thought possible after him.

There was a crinkle of a wrapper as he put on the condom he must have brought with him and, suddenly, she was on her feet, her legs spread only as wide as her panties would allow, and her front pressed to the linens.

"Hold on," he growled.

She held on.

Then he was inside of her, pumping in and out of her wet heat as she arched into him, her butt pressed tightly to his hips. He reached between them, flicking his fingers over her clit as he sucked on her neck, and then she couldn't hold back anymore.

Kenzie came on him, her legs shaking with the force of her orgasm, and soon, he was following her, his muffled grunts against her neck making her even hotter for him.

She'd never done something so dangerous, and she was lost to the temptation.

When he pulled out, he disposed of the condom in one of the small trash bags stored in the closet and used a towel to clean them both. The fact that they'd both been mostly dressed as they did this had only made it hotter, and each of them having to adjust their ruffled clothing made her swoon just a bit more.

Swoon.

She'd freaking swooned for Dare Collins, and she knew right then and there that she'd fallen in love with him. Deep, abiding love that scared the crap out of her.

"We shouldn't have done this," he said quietly, and she froze.

"What?" How her voice didn't shake, she didn't know.

"We're at work, damn it. And I just fucked you like a rutting bull in a fucking closet."

Cold, she folded her arms over her chest. "I was right there with you and, by the way, we're still in the damn closet." She paused, wondering where the hell all of this had come from. "What is going on, Dare? Talk to me."

"There's just a lot of shit going on right now, Kenzie, and I think we're moving too fast."

She blinked, an odd hollowness in her chest cascading down her body. "Excuse me?"

His face was emotionless as he looked at her, and she wished to hell she could read him. He stood there as if he weren't breaking her, and she had no idea what was going on. "I'm not saying what we did was wrong necessarily, and you and I aren't wrong either. But between things going on with Nate, and then you with David, maybe we're complicating things by doing this."

She swallowed hard, raising her chin like she had that first morning. "This. As in having sex? Or do you mean something more? Because what are we, Dare? I know I should have asked long before this and talked to you about my feelings as well as asked about yours, but really? And what do you mean about Nate? You didn't tell me anything was going on when it comes to him, so how could I possibly know what you mean. And I don't know what you mean about David either. Are you blaming me for him coming here?"

Shock crossed his face, and it was the first time she'd seen emotion on him since he started talking. "What? No. I'm just saying there are a lot of complications right now and it's making things hard."

"Hard. What things, Dare? If you're going to act like this, you need to tell me why things suddenly need to be different."

"Because I miss my kid, all right? Monica might let us finally change the custody agreement so I get more time with him, but she was pretty clear that I needed to make sure I'm not playing around."

Part of her was so damn excited for him that he could possibly have Nate more in his life.

The other part of her wanted to either scream at him or cry.

"Playing around. Because that's what we're doing."

"That's what we decided at first, right? Just for now. Nothing too serious because neither one of us was ready for that."

She stood frozen, unsure how it had come to this. Everything he was saying was true, but yet it wasn't. It didn't make sense, and honestly, she wasn't sure she could deal with him right then.

"You know what? Don't. Don't do this." She tightened her

jaw and held up her hand. "If you want to end this because you have no feelings for me and *playing around* will harm your chances with your son then, apparently, I had no idea what we were doing all this time. Because you know what, Dare? I fell for you. I love you, damn it. I promised myself I wouldn't fall for you because I thought I'd had love once before and I made a huge mistake. I didn't want to do it again. But, somehow, I fell again and convinced myself you couldn't be a mistake. It was wrong of me not to tell you when my feelings started to change because, apparently, I just drew this out and now it's awkward. So go do what you need to do. Be serious and don't *play around*. I won't stand in your way."

She pushed past him, tears in her throat and stinging her eyes. And when she opened the door to walk away, he didn't hold her back.

He just stood there.

He didn't call her name.

Didn't tell her he loved her, too.

Didn't say a damn thing.

She'd been wrong. So damn wrong.

And she only had herself to blame.

17

"**D**ARE, YOU'RE A fucking idiot," Fox said loudly from his stool at the bar. They were closed for the evening since it was a weeknight and they shut down a bit early but, apparently, Fox wanted to let the block know his feelings.

Dare stood on the other side of the bar cleaning glasses so he had something to do with his hands. Loch sat next to Fox, not drinking, but shooting his best glare in Dare's direction.

"I know I'm a fucking idiot," Dare spit out. "Why are you yelling it at me?"

"Seems to me you don't get it, so I'm yelling." Fox sipped his whiskey but didn't take his eyes off Dare. "What the fuck happened?"

"She left me. That's it." Now that was a damn lie, but Dare couldn't put his thoughts into words without growling.

"You're lying." Loch stared at the glass of water in his hands, but he was still talking to Dare.

"I'm not lying." Dare went back to cleaning glasses, his head lowered so he could focus on something mundane rather than his world crashing down around him. "She left."

"Yeah? And what did you do to facilitate that? What did you say? Because Kenzie fought so fucking hard to be where she is now, and I don't think she'd have walked away from something

189

that was *good* for her so quickly."

Dare looked up at Fox and frowned. "So it's my fault then?"

Yes.

"Yes," his brothers said in unison.

He dropped the glass in his hand into the soapy water, thankful he hadn't smashed it against the sink.

"Jesus, okay, fine. It's my fucking fault. And I have no idea how it got that way. My brain wasn't catching up to everything going on, and I kept saying the wrong damn things. I'm *still* saying the wrong damn thing."

"So, tell us," Fox demanded. "Maybe we can fix it."

"Not that either of us are role models for relationships," Loch added in.

"True, but maybe the three of us can figure this out." Fox shrugged. "You never know."

Dare studied his brothers and held back a sigh. Neither of them had been in many successful long-term relationships—including Loch's ex and Misty's mother—but they were always good at working with what they had and trying to find a solution to a problem.

"Monica told me she wants to try something different with custody and maybe give me more time."

"Are you serious?" Fox asked. "That's amazing."

"What's the catch?" Loch narrowed his eyes, and Dare sighed.

"She told me I needed to make sure that I knew what the fuck I was doing with Kenzie first. Because she's right, I can't hurt Nate by having Kenzie as a part of his life for long and then have her leave and fuck shit up for all of us."

"And you told Kenzie this, so she left?" Fox asked, confusion on his face.

Dare growled. "No. I didn't say anything. I'm a fucking idiot. Kenzie told me she loved me, and I said nothing. Nothing. Like my tongue had been cut off, or my mouth was sewn shut. I did nothing. Actually, no, I did say something. I told her that it was a mistake that we'd been sleeping together like we were and not figuring out what we were to each other. But I'm pretty sure the words came out like I thought everything we had done was a mistake. So I'm a damn idiot, and because my brain wasn't firing on all cylinders, I lost the woman I love."

Loch stood up, and without a word, walked around the bar. Fox just blinked up at both of them, and before Dare could take a breath, Loch punched him in the face.

"What the fuck, man?" Dare rubbed his jaw, grateful that Loch hadn't put much force behind it. "What was that for?"

"You're telling me you both love each other but she was the only one with the strength to say it? And then when she *did* say it, you let her walk out, thinking you don't feel anything for her except that it was a mistake? *And* you're telling me that you made her feel like she would be a hindrance in you getting to keep Nate for longer? Because that sounds like you're a dick. I might have to punch you again."

Dare held up his hands. "I know. *I know.* I was too much in my head, and I'm such a fucking idiot. When I was trying to think about what to do about Kenzie, I didn't know she felt that way about me. I. Didn't. Know. We both went into the relationship thinking we were in it for just the short-term and it would all be sex. I don't know when it changed for me, and I damn well didn't know it had changed for her." He paused. "No, that's not right either. I thought maybe it could have changed for her because of the way we slowly evolved, but I wasn't sure. And the fact that Monica came at me with this new idea, well, it fucked with my head. I was trying to make sure everything was coming together in my mind, but I was too slow to understand what I needed to say. I was honestly shocked when she told me she loved me. I didn't think she'd ever be able to love another person because of what had happened with her ex, yet she was way stronger than I was when it came to that. Hell, when it comes to anything. So, yes, I'm a damn idiot, and I *know* I need to try and fix this, but I have no idea how. I'm giving her space. It's been a fucking *day*, and I've tried to give her space. But all I want to do is go up there and make sure she knows I want her to be mine. Yet, at the same time, what right do I have? I hurt her, you guys. I fucking hurt her. What if I go up there and try to tell her what I feel and why I was so damn slow trying to explain what was going on in my head and I only hurt her more? Because I'd do anything not to hurt her again, yet I have a feeling no matter what I do, I'll keep hurting her because yeah, I'm a damn idiot."

Loch glowered down at him, while Fox blinked, his mouth opening and closing like a fish.

"That…that was a lot," Fox finally said.

"Yeah, yeah it was." Dare ran a hand over his face, wincing when he pressed his jaw. "And I don't know what to do."

"You love her." Loch's voice was low. "So go get on your knees and grovel for being an idiot and thinking with your dick and not your brain. There're no guests tonight since we're on that odd part of the year right before the big season starts, so go and make sure the woman you love knows you know you're a dumbass."

Fox slid down from his stool. "We'll head out. Finish cleaning and breathing so you can collect your thoughts and then go up and talk to your woman."

"Just don't be an asshole," Loch added before heading out of the bar with Fox at his side. That left Dare staring at the glasses in front of him, wondering what the hell he was going to do.

Why hadn't he said anything when she left?

Yeah, he'd been shocked speechless at first, but damn, he'd been screaming in his mind the whole time, yet he hadn't been able to move fast enough. He'd hurt her, and he'd never be able to forgive himself.

But he knew he couldn't live without her.

Dare blinked.

He couldn't live without her.

Sucking in a breath, he practically ran out of the bar and up the stairs. He'd thought Kenzie was at home, but she could be out since there were no guests. When he reached the door, he let out a slow breath before knocking.

He'd grovel.

He'd go down on his knees and beg.

He'd do anything to make sure that Kenzie knew she was worth far more than a man who couldn't get his head out of his ass long enough to make sure she knew she was loved and cared for. He'd do anything to prove that she was worth far more than him.

Kenzie opened the door, surprise on her face for a brief moment before she frowned. "Dare?"

And because all he could think of was the pain of not having her in his life, he did the only thing he could do.

He went to his knees. If there had been glass beneath his

skin, he'd have taken the punishment.

"I'm so fucking sorry, Kenzie. I should have said something. Hell, I should have said something from the beginning. I don't want to just be whatever we were. I started falling for you the first time you made me laugh. Hell, I think I knew there could be something between us the first moment you walked into my bar in that damn green dress that made your legs go on for miles."

"Dare..." She bit her lip and went to her knees in front of him. "You don't need to grovel. I left without letting you speak because I was afraid of what you would say. It's just as much my fault as it is yours. If I had talked to you *at all* about where my feelings were headed, maybe I wouldn't have freaked out like I did. You have Nate to think about, and because I was too scared about telling you how I felt or how I *could* feel, I made you think I didn't want more."

He cupped her face but didn't lean forward. "You shouldn't be on your knees, baby. You don't need to grovel to me. That's my job for you."

"No, we grovel for each other. And we *talk* to each other. Dare, I was so afraid of what I was feeling because of what happened with David that I almost didn't let myself feel. I should have told you. I should have talked to you. Instead, I almost walked away because I wasn't sure I deserved happiness. Or maybe it was because I was worried that since I'd made a mistake before, I would do it again. I don't know, really, but I do know that it was dumb of me to not tell you. Because since you didn't know, you couldn't be sure about where I fit in your life with Nate. And for that, I'm sorry."

Dare let out a harsh chuckle, shaking his head. "We're so

much alike sometimes, it's scary. Babe, if I was so worried about what would happen to my son with you in our lives, why didn't I just ask? Because I was a damn coward and scared about what the answer would be." He kept his hand on her cheek, this time leaning forward so their foreheads touched. "After losing Jason and all the crap that came with that, I almost felt like I didn't *deserve* the life that came with connecting with another person."

He paused so he could let his heart slow down just enough so he didn't hear the echo in his ears. It was hard to do that with her right in front of him, though.

"I love you, Kenzie. I love you so damn much. And I'm so fucking sorry I hurt you. But if you'll have me, I want to be in your life. I want you in *my* life. I want to tell you more about everything. And I want you to know Nate, too. I just want you, Kenzie. If you'll have me."

Tears slid down her cheeks, and she smiled. That smile was the best damn thing he'd seen in his life.

"I love you, too, Dare. And I want all of that, too. But from now on, we talk more." She snorted, and he grinned. "I need to know what you're feeling, and I need to be strong enough to tell you the same."

He kissed her then, needing her taste, her touch. "I can do that, Red. I *want* to do that."

He pulled her close, a little hard to do since they were still kneeling, and kissed her hard, their tongues slid against one another, and their lips moved in a passionate caress.

He was just about to stand them up when he froze, the scent of smoke on the air, filling his nostrils.

"What is that?" Kenzie asked, her face scrunching.

Dare stood quickly. "It smells like something's on fire."

Adrenaline pumping through his veins, he tugged on Kenzie's arm and pulled her downstairs. "No one else is here?"

Kenzie ran alongside him, barefoot and in her pajamas. "No guests, but I don't know about the restaurant or bar. What is going on? Where's the fire?"

"I don't fucking know where it is. I was the last person down here, but I'm getting you out." Smoke filled the air coming from the back of the building, so he pulled Kenzie out the front door. "I think it's coming from the back." He tossed her his cell phone. "Call 911. Someone might have spotted it already, but be sure. I'm going around back to see where the fire is coming from."

"I'm coming with you."

"You're barefoot."

"I don't care. You're not going alone."

Knowing it was not only useless to argue, but that they were running out of time, he started running, even as she was on the phone. As soon as they got to the back, he cursed.

Someone had broken one of the kitchen windows so smoke could billow into the building. The three trashcans beneath the window were on fire, flames and smoke pouring out of the plastic containers.

"Jesus."

"Oh my God." Kenzie was still on the line with 911, but she'd come right to his side. "They're already on their way, Dare."

"I need water. Or something. Shit. The building's not on fire yet, but that smoke is going to fuck everything up if we don't get it taken care of."

"You fucking bitch!"

Dare turned on his heel and tucked Kenzie behind him, his senses on alert. "Are you fucking kidding me, David? You started this shit?"

"David…" The anger in Kenzie's tone matched his own, though the surprise there made him want to kill the fucker for daring to come back and trying to hurt her.

Kenzie's ex stood on the other end of the small alley with a red gasoline container in his hand. Dare honestly couldn't believe what the fuck was going on, but he was done with people coming into his life and hurting those he loved.

He'd lost Jason because of an asshole.

He'd almost lost his kid because he'd been so lost.

And then he'd almost lost Kenzie for the same thing.

He wasn't about to let anyone touch Kenzie or the building he loved that was part of his family because some guy was an abusive asshole.

Sirens rang in the distance, and he knew the cops and fire trucks were on their way, but Dare only had eyes for David.

"Stay here," he growled at Kenzie, then ran toward David.

The other man stood there, his eyes wide with anger and a hint of insanity, but the man didn't move. Instead, he dropped the gas can, the empty tub making a hollow thump as it hit the concrete.

Dare punched the man in the face as hard as he could, and without a fight, David went down, out like a light. Dare would have thought it was anticlimactic, but his bar was on fire, and the love of his life was still near it.

Things moved quickly then.

Cops and ambulances made their way closer, and people started shouting. It was a small town, and others came, too, but

Dare only had eyes for Kenzie. He had her in his arms in an instant, bringing her in close.

Other members of his family had come, but he couldn't hear them.

Officers started speaking, and the firefighters took care of the fires quickly. Dare knew there would be questions. Knew there would be cleanup.

But he could only hold Kenzie.

Everything else could wait.

For once.

18

"THAT'S IT," DARE growled into her ear. "Take me."

Kenzie pushed back, arching into the man she loved as he pumped into her. He knelt behind her, fucking her hard as one hand slid over her clit, the other around her shoulders and neck.

"Show me," she gasped back. "Show me I'm yours."

He pounded into her, and she moved for him, meeting him thrust for thrust. When he bit her shoulder, that little growl of his echoing through her body, she came, her inner walls clenching around him.

He shook, filling her up as he came. She could feel the heat of him since they'd finally been able to forego a condom. She felt claimed.

His.

Dare's.

"Jesus, we need to do that again," Dare growled into her ear before trailing his lips over her skin. "I *knew* being bare inside you was going to be amazing, but I'm pretty sure I know why they call it the little death now."

They fell to their sides as he pulled out of her, and she turned in his arms, needing his touch. "I...I might need a minute before we do that again," she said with a laugh.

He gave a rough chuckle and pressed his lips to her temple. He couldn't quit touching her, and she loved it.

"I thought that would be my line."

She smiled, her eyes closed as she leaned into his touch. "We'll be ready again. Together. But first? Let's just cuddle." She laughed as she said it, and he held her close.

Dare hadn't been a cuddle guy before the fire, but now, they couldn't get enough of each other.

When they weren't working for the past few days, they'd either been talking or making love. She knew once they found their equilibrium they wouldn't be spending all of their free time—what little they had—in bed, but for now, she'd take all the time she could get with Dare.

"We should probably go downstairs at some point and see how the bar is doing," Dare said after a moment. He kept trailing his fingers over her skin as if he couldn't get enough of her. Considering that she couldn't get enough of him either, she didn't complain.

"True. Taking the afternoon off was nice, but I want to check in with the front desk and see how things are going." Since she'd first walked into Whiskey, she'd slowly been working on making the inn run smoother than it had when Barb and Bob ran it. They'd done amazing things, and with Kenzie's help, they'd been able to add two assistant innkeepers that really ran the place when Kenzie couldn't be there. The older couple was now able to retire, and Kenzie didn't have to work herself to the bone if she didn't want to.

And that was good because in the past three weeks since the fire, she'd been busy with everything else going on. David was still in jail, and she knew he'd be in there for a long time. Arson was only the tip of the iceberg when it came to what her ex had coming to him. She hadn't heard from her brother in all that time, and while it hurt her a bit that he didn't care enough to make sure she was okay, she knew it was for the best.

Maybe there would be time to reconcile later, but for now, she'd live her life the way she wanted to and not worry about those who wished her harm.

Her past was finally behind her, and though she felt horrible that her ex had tried to destroy something that was such a part of this town and the family she loved, she didn't blame herself.

Dare wouldn't let her.

It had taken almost losing everything important to her to realize that she was finally the Kenzie she was always meant to be.

"What are you thinking about so hard over there?" Dare asked as they were dressing to go downstairs.

"Just everything that's happened over the past few months." She met his gaze and saw his glower. "I'm happy, Dare. Things are good. You know?"

He nodded, but she knew he was still pissed off about everything that had happened. He didn't blame her, but he still told her that sometimes he wanted to kick her ex's ass again. Since she wanted to, as well, she couldn't blame him.

Instead of saying anything, he stalked over to her and brought her in for a demanding kiss. "I love you, Kenzie Owens. Fucking *love* you. Don't forget that."

Her toes curled just like they did every time he told her. "I won't. I love you, too, Dare. Now let's go downstairs and see what's going on in your bar. I could use some whiskey."

Dare grinned. "Yeah, that's my girl. Whiskey and having you

near me? I'm a pretty lucky man."

She patted his chest before reaching down to slip on her shoes. "And don't you forget it."

She'd found her happiness when she hadn't been looking or actively fighting against it. She had friends, a home to call her own, a job she loved, and a man she would never take for granted.

Her path wasn't over, far from it. There were still twists and turns coming, she knew that, but she also knew this wasn't the end. She no longer needed to hide her secrets in order to survive. Her past didn't hold her down any longer.

Nothing did.

Epilogue

DARE WAS ONE lucky man. He'd spent the morning on the phone with his son, talking about what they were going to do next week when they had seven full days together. Then he'd spent the afternoon wrapped around Kenzie. And now, he was hanging out with his family, friends, and the woman he loved in the bar that called to his soul.

Somehow, through all the fuck-ups and mistakes he'd made over the past few years, everything had come full circle.

And hell, he was *happy*.

He'd just gotten off the phone with Monica before walking back into the bar and couldn't keep from smiling. The two of them were going to work out a new joint custody agreement because like he'd said all along, Monica was a damn good mother. And now that he could think clearly, he knew he was a damn good father, as well. Figuring out the balance for Nate over the next few months would be tricky, but they were going to make it work. Dare and Monica lived in the same school district and were going to do their best to be open and honest about what was working and what wasn't. Their lawyers would be involved for paperwork's sake, but they were going to make things work between them no matter what.

Dare would have his kid in his life more than a few hours a

month and he couldn't be happier.

"You look happy," his mom said as she walked up to him. "I'm glad to see it."

He leaned down and hugged her close. "I *am* happy."

"Good. Seems to me, hiring that innkeeper was a good idea."

He rolled his eyes, remembering how much of an asshole he'd been. "You were right."

"That's your mother's favorite thing to hear," his dad added as he walked up.

Dare just smiled and let them razz him a bit. He deserved it for being such an ass. After they'd finished talking about what they were going to do next weekend with him and Nate, Dare went over to the corner booth where Kenzie, Ainsley, and Jesse were talking and tasting a new whiskey flight Dare had worked up.

"Doing good, ladies?" he asked before dropping a kiss on Kenzie's temple.

She grinned up at him and saluted with her drink. "Yep. I think this one's my favorite. It's the barrel one, right?"

He studied it and nodded. "Yeah, it's pretty smoky. I like it, too." He leaned down again and kissed her lips, the taste of whiskey on her tongue making him hard…though that bit was probably just Kenzie.

"You guys are disgustingly cute," Jesse said with a laugh. "I wonder if Rob and I are that cute."

Jesse had started seeing a new man, an accountant of all things, about a month ago, and Dare couldn't be happier for her. She was smiling more than she ever had before, and he was glad she was finally healing like he was. It had taken them a while, and he knew they still had a ways to go, but they weren't the same person they were when Jason died.

And Dare never once ignored her calls. He wasn't that man anymore.

"Probably cuter," Kenzie answered.

"Hey," Dare said, affronted. "I'm right here."

"Yes, you are. And I love you."

He just shook his head and leaned against the side of the booth. "Doing okay over there, Ainsley?"

The other woman nodded, a frown on her face as she studied her phone. "Yeah, just trying to catch up on emails while I do this. I think there needs to be more hours in the day."

"I can't argue with you there." Dare frowned and looked around the bar. "I thought Loch would be here?"

Ainsley looked up quickly. "Your parents wanted a night out, so Loch's home with Misty. I offered to watch her, but he said he was fine." She shrugged as she said it, but Dare caught something in her tone. He looked over at Kenzie, who shook her head. Maybe there was something going on there, or maybe Dare was just looking too hard into things. He honestly didn't know anymore.

He turned away from the booth slightly and looked over at the bar, a smile playing on his lips. "Who's the blonde at the bar with Fox?"

Ainsley looked around him, and Dare ran his hand through Kenzie's hair, unable to stop touching her. "No clue, but she's hot."

"And getting tipsy," Jesse put in. "Your brother's pretty tipsy, too, I think."

Dare frowned. "Should I cut them off?" He shook his head. "I'll go talk to Rick in a bit and see how much they've had."

"Overprotective," Ainsley teased.

"Hell yeah, I am. Can't help it. Oh, that reminds me, Tabby said she was going to call you tomorrow about wedding stuff." The wedding was coming up soon, and Dare had told his sister that he was bringing Kenzie and Nate along. To say his baby sister was thrilled was an understatement.

"Sounds good to me. I can't wait to meet her." Kenzie smiled up at him.

"I can't wait for you to meet her either." He leaned down and took her lips in a deep kiss, ignoring the laughs from Ainsley and Jesse.

He'd gone through his life from point to point, barely scraping by emotionally as he tried to find his place in the world, and had almost lost everything more than once. It had taken him finally opening up and thinking about what he wanted for him to take that chance and find exactly what he'd always dreamed of.

A family he grew closer to with each passing year.

A small town that took care of its own.

A son that was the light of his world.

A business that called to him.

And a woman that he wanted in his life until the end of his days.

Kenzie was his future, and damned if he didn't love the idea of growing old with her. One unveiled secret at a time.

Up Next:

Fox meets Melody in WHISKEY REVEALS

A Note from Carrie Ann

Thank you so much for reading **WHISKEY SECRETS**. I do hope if you liked this story, that you would please leave a review! Reviews help authors *and* readers.

I so hope you enjoyed Dare and Kenzie's story and cannot wait for you to find out more about the other two brothers. I'm loving this world and going back to write about them when I had to put them aside for too long was a true dream.

Next up is Fox and Melody and after that, Loch and Ainsley get their romance! And if you're new to my books, this series is also part of a bigger world though they are all stand alone, so you have a ton of books to fall in love with!

Don't miss out on the Montgomery Ink World!

- Montgomery Ink (The Denver Montgomerys)
- Montgomery Ink: Colorado Springs (The Colorado Springs Montgomery Cousins)
- Gallagher Brothers (Jake's Brothers from Ink Enduring)
- Whiskey and Lies (Tabby's Brothers from Ink Exposed)

If you want to make sure you know what's coming next from me, you can sign up for my newsletter at www.CarrieAnnRyan.com; follow me on twitter at @CarrieAnnRyan, or like my Facebook page. I also have a Facebook Fan Club where we have trivia, chats, and other goodies. You guys are the reason I get to do what I do and I thank you.

Make sure you're signed up for my MAILING LIST so you can know when the next releases are available as well as find giveaways and FREE READS.

Happy Reading!

The Whiskey and Lies Series:
A Montgomery Ink Spin Off Series
Book 1: Whiskey Secrets
Book 2: Whiskey Reveals (Coming June 2018)
Book 3: Whiskey Undone (Coming Oct 2018)

Want to keep up to date with the next Carrie Ann Ryan Release?
Receive Text Alerts easily!
Text CARRIE to 24587

About Carrie Ann

Carrie Ann Ryan is the New York Times and USA Today bestselling author of contemporary and paranormal romance. Her works include the Montgomery Ink, Redwood Pack, Talon Pack, and Gallagher Brothers series, which have sold over 2.0 million books worldwide. She started writing while in graduate school for her advanced degree in chemistry and hasn't stopped since. Carrie Ann has written over fifty novels and novellas with more in the works. When she's not writing about bearded tattooed men or alpha wolves that need to find their mates, she's reading as much as she can and exploring the world of baking and gourmet cooking.

www.CarrieAnnRyan.com

More from Carrie Ann

Montgomery Ink:
Book 0.5: Ink Inspired
Book 0.6: Ink Reunited
Book 1: Delicate Ink
Book 1.5: Forever Ink
Book 2: Tempting Boundaries
Book 3: Harder than Words
Book 4: Written in Ink
Book 4.5: Hidden Ink
Book 5: Ink Enduring
Book 6: Ink Exposed
Book 6.5: Adoring Ink
Book 6.6: Love, Honor, & Ink
Book 7: Inked Expressions
Book 7.5: Executive Ink
Book 8: Inked Memories

Montgomery Ink: Colorado Springs
Book 1: Fallen Ink (Coming Apr 2018)
Book 2: Restless Ink (Coming Aug 2018)

The Gallagher Brothers Series:
A Montgomery Ink Spin Off Series
Book 1: Love Restored
Book 2: Passion Restored
Book 3: Hope Restored

The Whiskey and Lies Series:
A Montgomery Ink Spin Off Series
Book 1: Whiskey Secrets

Book 2: Whiskey Reveals (Coming June 2018)
Book 3: Whiskey Undone (Coming Oct 2018)

The Talon Pack:
Book 1: Tattered Loyalties
Book 2: An Alpha's Choice
Book 3: Mated in Mist
Book 4: Wolf Betrayed
Book 5: Fractured Silence
Book 6: Destiny Disgraced
Book 7: Eternal Mourning (Coming Feb 2018)
Book 8: Strength Enduring (Coming July 2018)
Book 9: Forever Broken (Coming in 2019)

Redwood Pack Series:
Prequel: An Alpha's Path
Book 1: A Taste for a Mate
Book 2: Trinity Bound
Book 2.5: A Night Away
Book 3: Enforcer's Redemption
Book 3.5: Blurred Expectations
Book 3.7: Forgiveness
Book 4: Shattered Emotions
Book 5: Hidden Destiny
Book 5.5: A Beta's Haven
Book 6: Fighting Fate
Book 6.5: Loving the Omega
Book 6.7: The Hunted Heart
Book 7: Wicked Wolf
The Complete Redwood Pack Box Set (Contains Books 1-7.7)

The Branded Pack Series:
(Written with Alexandra Ivy)
Book 1: Stolen and Forgiven
Book 2: Abandoned and Unseen
Book 3: Buried and Shadowed

Dante's Circle Series:
Book 1: Dust of My Wings
Book 2: Her Warriors' Three Wishes
Book 3: An Unlucky Moon
Book 3.5: His Choice
Book 4: Tangled Innocence
Book 5: Fierce Enchantment
Book 6: An Immortal's Song
Book 7: Prowled Darkness
The Complete Dante's Circle Series (Contains Books 1-7)

Holiday, Montana Series:
Book 1: Charmed Spirits
Book 2: Santa's Executive
Book 3: Finding Abigail
Book 4: Her Lucky Love
Book 5: Dreams of Ivory
The Complete Holiday, Montana Box Set (Contains Books 1-5)

Stand Alone Romances:
Finally Found You
Flame and Ink
Ink Ever After
Dropout

Delicate Ink

"**I**F YOU DON'T turn that fucking music down, I'm going to ram this tattoo gun up a place no one on this earth should ever see."

Austin Montgomery lifted the needle from his client's arm so he could hold back a rough chuckle. He let his foot slide off the pedal so he could keep his composure. Dear Lord, his sister Maya clearly needed more coffee in her life.

Or for someone to turn down the fucking music in the shop.

"You're not even working, Maya. Let me have my tunes," Sloane, another artist, mumbled under his breath. Yeah, he didn't yell it. Didn't need to. No one wanted to yell at Austin's sister. The man might be as big as a house and made of pure muscle, but no one messed with Maya.

Not if they wanted to live.

"I'm sketching, you dumbass," Maya sniped, even though the smile in her eyes belied her wrath. His sister loved Sloane like a brother. Not that she didn't have enough brothers and sisters to begin with, but the Montgomerys always had their arms open for strays and spares.

Austin rolled his eyes at the pair's antics and stood up from his stool, his body aching from being bent over for too long. He refrained from saying that aloud as Maya and Sloane would have a joke for that. He usually preferred to have the other person in bed—or in the kitchen, office, doorway, etc—bent over, but that wasn't where he would allow his mind to go. As it was, he was too damn old to be sitting in that position for too long, but he wanted to get this sleeve done for his customer.

"Hold on a sec, Rick," he said to the man in the chair. "Want juice or anything? I'm going to stretch my legs and make sure Maya doesn't kill Sloane." He winked as he said it, just in case his client didn't get the joke.

People could be so touchy when siblings threatened each other with bodily harm even while they smiled as they said it.

"Juice sounds good," Rick slurred, a sappy smile on his face. "Don't let Maya kill you."

Rick blinked his eyes open, the adrenaline running through his system giving him the high that a few patrons got once they were in the chair for a couple hours. To Austin, there was nothing better than having Maya ink his skin—or doing it himself—and letting the needle do its work. He wasn't a pain junkie, far from it if he was honest with himself, but he liked the adrenaline that led the way into fucking fantastic art. While some people thought bodies were sacred and tattoos only marred them, he knew it differently. Art on canvas, any canvas, could have the potential to be art worth bleeding for. As such, he was particular as to who laid a needle on his skin. He only let Maya ink him when he couldn't do it himself. Maya was the same way. Whatever she couldn't do herself, he did.

They were brother and sister, friends, and co-owners of Montgomery Ink.

He and Maya had opened the shop a decade ago when she'd turned twenty. He probably could have opened it a few years earlier since he was eight years older than Maya, but he'd wanted to wait until she was ready. They were joint owners. It had never been his shop while she worked with him. They both had equal say, although with the way Maya spoke, sometimes her voice seemed louder. His deeper one carried just as much weight, even if he didn't yell as much.

Barely.

Sure, he wasn't as loud as Maya, but he got his point across when needed. His voice held control and authority.

He picked up a juice box for Rick from their mini-fridge and turned down the music on his way back. Sloane scowled at him, but the corner of his mouth twitched as if he held back a laugh.

"Thank God one of you has a brain in his head," Maya mumbled in the now quieter room. She rolled her eyes as both he and Sloane flipped her off then went back to her sketch. Yeah, she could have gotten up to turn the music down herself, but then she couldn't have vented her excess energy at the two of them. That was just how his sister worked, and there would be no changing that.

He went back to his station situated in the back so he had the corner space, handed Rick his juice, then rubbed his back. Damn, he was getting old. Thirty-eight wasn't that far up there on the scales, but ever since he'd gotten back from New Orleans, he hadn't been able to shake the weight of something off of his chest.

He needed to be honest. He'd started feeling this way since before New Orleans. He'd gone down to the city to visit his cousin Shep and try to get out of his funk. He'd broken up with Shannon right before then; however, in reality, it wasn't as much a breakup as a lack of connection and communication. They hadn't cared about each other enough to move on to the next level, and as sad as that was, he was fine with it. If he couldn't get up the energy to pursue a woman beyond a couple of weeks or months of heat, then he knew he was the problem. He just didn't know the solution. Shannon hadn't been the first woman who had ended the relationship in that fashion. There'd been Brenda, Sandrine, and another one named Maggie.

He'd cared for all of them at the time. He wasn't a complete asshole, but he'd known deep down that they weren't going to be with him forever, and they thought the same of him. He also knew that it was time to actually find a woman to settle down with. If he wanted a future, a family, he was running out of time.

Going to New Orleans hadn't worked out in the least considering, at the time, Shep was falling in love with a pretty blonde named Shea. Not that Austin begrudged the man that. Shep had been his best friend growing up, closer to him than his four brothers and three sisters. It'd helped that he and Shep were the same age while the next of his siblings, the twins Storm and Wes, were four years younger.

His parents had taken their time to have eight kids, meaning he was a full fifteen years older than the baby, Miranda, but he hadn't cared. The eight of them, most of his cousins, and a few strays were as close as ever. He'd helped raise the youngest ones as an older brother but had never felt like he had to. His parents, Marie and Harry, loved each of their kids equally and had put their whole beings into their roles as parents. Every single concert, game, ceremony, or even parent-teacher meeting was attended by at least one of them. On the good days, the ones where Dad could get off work and Mom had the day off from Montgomery Inc., they both would attend. They loved their kids.

He loved being a Montgomery.

The sound of Sloane's needle buzzing as he sang whatever tune played in his head made Austin grin.

And he fucking *loved* his shop.

Every bare brick and block of polished wood, every splash of black and hot pink—colors he and Maya had fought on and he'd eventually given in to—made him feel at home. He'd taken the family crest and symbol, the large MI surrounded by a broken floral circle, and used it as their logo. His brothers, Storm and Wes, owned Montgomery Inc., a family construction company that their father had once owned and where their mother had worked at his side before they'd retired. They, too, used the same logo since it meant family to them.

In fact, the MI was tattooed on every single immediate family member—including his parents. His own was on his right forearm tangled in the rest of his sleeve but given a place of meaning. It meant Montgomery Iris—*open your eyes, see the beauty, remember who you are.* It was only natural to use it for their two respective companies.

Not that the Ink vs Inc. wasn't confusing as hell, but fuck, they were Montgomerys. They could do whatever they wanted. As long as they were together, they'd get through it.

Montgomery Ink was just as much his home as his house on the ravine. While Shep had gone on to work at Midnight Ink and created another family there, Austin had always wanted to own his shop. Maya growing up to want to do the same thing had only helped.

Montgomery Ink was now a thriving business in downtown Denver right off 16th Street Mall. They were near parking, food, and coffee. There really wasn't more he needed. The drive in most mornings could suck once he got on I-25, but it was worth it to live out in Arvada. The 'burbs around Denver made it easy to live in one area of the city and work in another. Commutes, though hellish at rush hour, weren't as bad as some. This way he got the city living when it came to work and play, and the option to hide behind the trees pressed up against the foothills of the Rocky Mountains once he got home.

It was the best of both worlds.

At least for him.

Austin got back on his stool and concentrated on Rick's sleeve for another hour before calling it quits. He needed a break for his lower back, and Rick needed a break from the pain. Not that Rick was feeling much since the man currently looked like he'd just gotten laid—pain freaks, Austin loved them—but he didn't want to push either of them too far. Also, Plus Rick's arm had started to swell slightly from all the shading and multiple colors. They'd do another session, the last, hopefully, in a month or so when both of them could work it in their schedules and then finish up.

Austin scowled at the computer at the front of shop, his fingers too big for the damn keys on the prissy computer Maya had demanded they buy.

"Fuck!"

He'd just deleted Rick's whole account because he couldn't find the right button.

"Maya, get your ass over here and fix this. I don't know what the hell I did."

Maya lifted one pierced brow as she worked on a lower back tattoo for some teenage girl who didn't look old enough to get ink in the first place.

"I'm busy, Austin. You're not an idiot, though evidence at

the moment points to the contrary. Fix it yourself. I can't help it if you have ape hands."

Austin flipped her off then took a sip of his Coke, wishing he had something stronger considering he hated paperwork. "I was fine with the old keyboard and the PC, Maya. You're the one who wanted to go with the Mac because it looked pretty."

"Fuck you, Austin. I wanted a Mac because I like the software."

Austin snorted while trying to figure out how to find Rick's file. He was pretty sure it was a lost cause at this point. "You hate the software as much as I do. You hit the damn red X and close out files more than I do. Everything's in the wrong place, and the keyboard is way too fucking dainty."

"I'm going to go with Austin on this one," Sloane added in, his beefy hands in the air.

"See? I'm not alone."

Maya let out a breath. "We can get another keyboard for you and Gigantor's hands, but we need to keep the Mac."

"And why is that?" he demanded.

"Because we just spent a whole lot of money on it, and once it goes, we can get another PC. Fuck the idea that everything can be all in one. I can't figure it out either." She held up a hand. "And don't even think about breaking it. I'll know, Austin. I *always* know."

Austin held back a grin. He wouldn't be surprised if the computer met with an earlier than expected unfortunate fate now that Maya had relented.

Right then, however, that idea didn't help. He needed to find Rick's file.

"Callie!" Austin yelled over the buzz of needles and soft music Maya had allowed them to play.

"What?" His apprentice came out of the break room, a sketchbook in one hand and a smirk on her face. She'd dyed her hair again so it had black and red highlights. It looked good on her, but honestly, he never knew what color she'd have next. "Break something on the computer again with those big man hands?"

"Shut up, minion," he teased. Callie was an up-and-coming artist, and if she kept on the track she was on, he and Maya knew she'd be getting her own chair at Montgomery Ink soon. Not that he'd tell Callie that, though. He liked keeping her on her toes. She reminded him of his little sister Miranda so much that he couldn't help but treat her as such.

She pushed him out of the way and groaned. "Did you have to press *every* button as you rampaged through the operating system?"

Austin could have sworn he felt his cheeks heat, but since he had a thick enough beard, he knew no one would have been able to tell.

Hopefully.

He hated feeling as if he didn't know what he was doing. It wasn't as if he didn't know how to use a computer. He wasn't an idiot. He just didn't know *this* computer. And it bugged the shit out of him.

After a couple of keystrokes and a click of the mouse, Callie stepped back with a smug smile on her face. "Okay, boss, you're all ready to go, and Rick's file is back where it should be. What else do you need from me?"

He bopped her on the head, messing up her red and black hair he knew she spent an hour on every morning with a flat iron. He couldn't help it.

"Go clean a toilet or something."

Callie rolled her eyes. "I'm going to go sketch. And you're welcome."

"Thanks for fixing the damn thing. And really, go clean the bathroom."

"Not gonna do it," she sang as she skipped to the break room.

"You really have no control over your apprentice," Sloane commented from his station.

Because he didn't want that type of control with her. Well, hell, his mind kept going to that dark place every few minutes it seemed.

"Shut up, asshole."

"I see your vocabulary hasn't changed much," Shannon purred from the doorway.

He closed his eyes and prayed for patience. Okay, maybe he'd lied to himself when he said it was mutual and easy to break up with her. The damn woman kept showing up. He didn't think she wanted him, but she didn't want him to forget her either.

He did not understand women.

Especially this one.

"What do you want, Shannon?" he bit out, needing that drink now more than ever.

She sauntered over to him and scraped her long, red nail down his chest. He'd liked that once. Now, not even a little. They were decent together when they'd dated, but he'd had to hide most of himself from her. She'd never tasted the edge of his flogger or felt his hand on her ass when she'd been bent over his lap. That hadn't been what she wanted, and Austin was into the kind of kink that meant he wanted what he wanted when he wanted. It didn't mean he wanted it every time.

Not that Shannon would ever understand that.

"Oh, baby, you know what I want."

He barely resisted the urge to roll his eyes. As he took a step back, he saw the gleam in her eyes and decided to head it off at the pass. He was in no mood to play her games, or whatever she wanted to do that night. He wanted to go home, drink a beer, and forget this oddly annoying day.

"If you don't want ink, then I don't know what you're doing here, Shannon. We're done." He tried to say it quietly, but his voice was deep, and it carried.

"How could you be so cruel?" She pouted.

"Oh, for the love of God," Maya sneered. "Go home, little girl. You and Austin are through, and I'm pretty sure it was mutual. Oh, and you're not getting any ink here. You're not getting Austin's hands on you this way, and there's no way in hell I'm putting my art on you. Not if you keep coming back to bug the man you didn't really date in the first place."

"Bi—" Shannon cut herself off as Austin glared. Nobody called his sister a bitch. Nobody.

"Goodbye, Shannon." Jesus, he was too old for this shit.

"Fine. I see how it is. Whatever. You were only an okay lay anyway." She shook her ass as she left, bumping into a woman in a linen skirt and blouse.

The woman, whose long honey-brown hair hung in waves down to her breasts, raised a brow. "I see your business has an...interesting clientele."

Austin clenched his jaw. Seriously the wrong thing to say

after Shannon.

"If you've got a problem, you can head on right back to where you came from, Legs," he bit out, his voice harsher than he'd intended.

She stiffened then raised her chin, a clear sense of disdain radiating off of her.

Oh yes, he knew who this was, legs and all. Ms. Elder. He hadn't caught a first name. Hadn't wanted to. She had to be in her late twenties, maybe, and owned the soon-to-be-opened boutique across the street. He'd seen her strut around in her too-tall heels and short skirts but hadn't been formally introduced.

Not that he wanted an introduction.

She was too damn stuffy and ritzy for his taste. Not only her store but the woman herself. The look of disdain on her face made him want to show her the door and never let her back in.

He knew what he looked like. Longish dark brown hair, thick beard, muscles covered in ink with a hint of more ink coming out of his shirt. He looked like a felon to some people who didn't know the difference, though he'd never seen the inside of a jail cell in his life. But he knew people like Ms. Elder. They judged people like him. And that one eyebrow pissed him the fuck off.

He didn't want this woman's boutique across the street from him. He'd liked it when it was an old record store. People didn't glare at his store that way. Now he had to walk past the mannequins with the rich clothes and tiny lacy scraps of things if he wanted a fucking coffee from the shop next door.

Damn it, this woman pissed him off, and he had no idea why.

"Nice to meet you too. Callie!" he shouted, his eyes still on

Ms. Elder as if he couldn't pull his gaze from her. Her green eyes never left his either, and the uncomfortable feeling in his gut wouldn't go away.

Callie ran up beside him and held out her hand. "Hi, I'm Callie. How can I help you?"

Ms. Elder blinked once. Twice. "I think I made a mistake," she whispered.

Fuck. Now he felt like a heel. He didn't know what it was with this woman, but he couldn't help but act like an ass. She hadn't even done anything but lift an eyebrow at him, and he'd already set out to hate her.

Callie shook her head then reached for Ms. Elder's elbow. "I'm sure you haven't. Ignore the growly, bearded man over there. He needs more caffeine. And his ex was just in here; that alone would make anyone want to jump off the Royal Gorge. So, tell me, how can I help you? Oh! And what's your name?"

Ms. Elder followed Callie to the sitting area with leather couches and portfolios spread over the coffee table and then sat down.

"I'm Sierra, and I want a tattoo." She looked over her shoulder and glared at Austin. "Or, at least, I thought I did."

Austin held back a wince when she turned her attention from him and cursed himself. Well, fuck. He needed to learn not to put his foot in his mouth, but damn it, how was he supposed to know she wanted a tattoo? For all he knew, she wanted to come in there and look down on the place. That was his own prejudice coming into play. He needed to make it up to her. After all, they were neighbors now. However, from the cross look on her face and the feeling in the room, he knew that he wasn't going to be able to make it up to her today. He'd let Callie help her out to start with, and then he'd make sure he was the one who laid ink on her skin.

After all, it was the least he could do. Besides, his hands all of a sudden—or not so suddenly if he really thought about it—wanted to touch that delicate skin of hers and find out her secrets.

Austin cursed. He wouldn't let his thoughts go down that path. She'd break under his care, under his needs. Sure, Sierra Elder might be hot, but she wasn't the woman for him.

If he knew anything, he knew *that* for sure.

Find out more in Delicate Ink. **Out Now.**
To make sure you're up to date on all of Carrie Ann's releases, sign up for her mailing list HERE.
bit.ly/18aFEqP

Love Restored

In the first of a Montgomery Ink spin-off series from NYT Bestselling Author Carrie Ann Ryan, a broken man uncovers the truth of what it means to take a second chance with the most unexpected woman…

Graham Gallagher has seen it all. And when tragedy struck, lost it all. He's been the backbone of his brothers, the one they all rely on in their lives and business. And when it comes to falling in love and creating a life, he knows what it's like to have it all and watch it crumble. He's done with looking for another person to warm his bed, but apparently he didn't learn his lesson because the new piercer at Montgomery Ink tempts him like no other.

Blake Brennen may have been born a trust fund baby, but she's created a whole new life for herself in the world of ink, piercings, and freedom. Only the ties she'd thought she'd cut long ago aren't as severed as she'd believed. When she finds Graham constantly in her path, she knows from first glance that he's the wrong kind of guy for her. Except that Blake excels at making the wrong choice and Graham might be the ultimate temptation for the bad girl she'd thought long buried.

Find out more in Love Restored. **Out Now.**
To make sure you're up to date on all of Carrie Ann's releases, sign up for her mailing list HERE.
bit.ly/18aFEqP

Tattered Loyalties

When the great war between the Redwoods and the Centrals occurred three decades ago, the Talon Pack risked their lives for the side of good. After tragedy struck, Gideon Brentwood became the Alpha of the Talons. But the Pack's stability is threatened, and he's forced to take mate—only the one fate puts in his path is the woman he shouldn't want.

Though the daughter of the Redwood Pack's Beta, Brie Jamenson has known peace for most of her life. When she finds the man who could be her mate, she's shocked to discover Gideon is the Alpha wolf of the Talon Pack. As a submissive, her strength lies in her heart, not her claws. But if her new Pack disagrees or disapproves, the consequences could be fatal.

As the worlds Brie and Gideon have always known begin to shift, they must face their challenges together in order to help their Pack and seal their bond. But when the Pack is threatened from the inside, Gideon doesn't know who he can trust and Brie's life could be forfeit in the crossfire. It will take the strength of an Alpha and the courage of his mate to realize where true loyalties lie.

Find out more in Tattered Loyalties. **Out Now.**
To make sure you're up to date on all of Carrie Ann's
releases, sign up for her mailing list HERE.
bit.ly/18aFEqP